Care and Feeding of Your Little Banned Bookshop

Jennifer Shelby

ISBN: 978-1-7386696-5-3

Content Warning:

Homophobia, Transphobia

Religious trauma, Evangelism

Domestic abuse

for the books

(and those who need them)

Of all stories written and told, of all books banned and hidden away, the story of this Bookshop had hoped it would find you. You have been trusted with these pages, the lifeblood of the Little Banned Bookshop, and should consider yourself honored indeed.

CONTENTS

CHAPTER 1

That's the thing about magic Bookshops, they're not around if they're not needed. They could be elsewhere, some place they are needed, or they could be enjoying the respite, using the downtime to gather their strength and renew their stock.

Once in a very long while, a Little Banned Bookshop without a Shopkeeper may grow dormant. If you've been assigned such a Bookshop, please understand that your Bookshop may experience some disorientation as they return to service. This may present itself as confusion, internal disarray, and, in some cases, clinginess. This can be disconcerting for a new Shopkeeper, but we can assure you, the disorientation is only temporary and your Bookshop will be in top condition in no time. Just remember to reassure your Bookshop that they are not alone and you're there to look after them.

-Care and Feeding of Your Little Banned Bookshop, pages 1-2

Gabby watched the boy pull out his phone and smile down at it, momentarily forgetting that he was supposed to be helping her load the empty sod pallets onto the utility trailer. "I've seen that look before. Have you met some-one?"

Talon's cheeks flamed as he tucked the phone away. "Maybe. I haven't known them long. I like them, but... I dunno. They're not really out." Talon used air quotes to signify his meaning. "I guess their parents are very re-ligious."

Gabby hefted a pallet onto the trailer. "They can't con-trol their parents. I grew up in an evangelical household myself." *Cult,* she mentally corrected herself. But Talon didn't want to hear that story.

Talon brightened. "Yeah, I suppose you're right. Just seems like they're always in trouble."

It's all about control. "Sounds like they probably need all the support they can get."

"Yeah." Talon stared thoughtfully into the distance.

Gabby liked the kid--*but gosh*--she wished he could think and work at the same time. "You know, my daughter Ashlin works at the youth center on Tenth. It's a safe place, if they ever need one."

Talon reached for a pallet and held it in his arms. "Does she volunteer after school?"

Gabby chuckled. "Nah, she's grown and on her own. Has a degree in social work. She's always wanted to help kids in need."

"Wow, you must be really proud of her." At last, he added the pallet to the trailer.

"I am." Gabby smiled to herself. *So proud.* "You strap down the pallets, I'll go let the client know the sprinkler schedule." She wiped the worst of the dirt from laying sod all day on her pants and left Talon to fumble with the straps. At least her t-shirt had escaped much of the day's mess. *Mulvaney Landscaping*, it announced. A business card for folks who got their hands dirty.

It wasn't any of her business, but Gabby couldn't help but think of the kid as she drove home later. Their situation seemed so similar to what hers had been. She wished she lived in a world where people didn't have to be afraid to be themselves.

When she pulled into the driveway, her best friend and roommate, Manny, was pulling weeds in the front garden, a sure sign he needed alone time. Gabby waved and went inside, her thoughts drifting back to those hard years in the Beholders cult.

The first thing Gabby allowed herself to believe in after she escaped the fundamentalist cult was magic. Magic was a dirty word in the Christian circles she'd been trapped in, even if a lot of religious elements looked like magic. Smelled like magic. Heck, most of them worked like magic, too.

Magic defied bounds. It didn't pay any attention to rules at all. That's why Gabby loved it and why the Beholders insisted it didn't exist and banned any books about magic. Rules were everything to them.

She peered out the kitchen window, across the yard, to Gabby and Manny's Little Free Library. For Leona, it read on the side, beside a small Trans flag. She could almost see one of the Beholder's evangelists now, glaring at the books.

Gabby frowned. No, this well-manicured, blonde woman digging through the book cupboard was real. She just reminded Gabby of the Beholders.

Gabby hesitated. She'd been a frumpy, middle-aged, introverted mother of a grown daughter for long enough to enjoy the invisibility such qualities bequeathed to her. Once she engaged this woman, she would lose the protection of that invisibility, and judging by the daggers the woman stared into the wooden library cupboard, Gabby doubted she'd enjoy this woman seeing her.

She glanced over to her housemate, Manny. He knelt in the begonias, his pink clippers held in suspended animation, about to clip a damaged leaf, his attention caught up by the anti-gravity of this woman as well.

Rachel Forrest, Gabby realized, as she stepped outside and into the front yard. This must be the matriarch of the new family who'd moved in at the far end of the street. She remembered the name because--Rachel Forrest--now THAT was a main character name if she'd ever heard one. Seeing her in person, Gabby had to admit some disappointment that rather than a main character, Rachel Forrest reminded Gabby of her mother.

Her right hand curled instinctively, searching for the old skeleton key that, once upon a time, she never took off. It wasn't there, it was safely stowed in a wooden box on her dresser, and she felt a fierce stab of longing for the comfort it could have given her if she had been wearing it.

"Hi there. You're Rachel, right? Your family moved in last month?" Gabby forced a friendliness into her tone as she approached the woman.

Rachel's washed-out blue eyes fixed themselves on Gabby's brown ones and, within the space of that millisecond, Gabby's protective invisibility crumbled. Rather than answering Gabby's friendly tone with her own, Rachel bared her teeth and tossed a black-and-white paperback into Gabby's face.

Gabby caught the thing just before it connected with her nose, instinctively searching for the title. Kate Bornstein's *Hello Cruel World: 101 Alternatives to Suicide for Teens, Freaks, and other Outlaws*. A soft wave of fondness for the book washed over Gabby. This book was always disappearing from the Little Free Library. She and Manny had no less than five copies in the house at this moment. It was one of the main reasons they kept the Little Free Library up all these years: the hope that this book could make a difference to some kid who needed it.

Rachel still glared at Gabby, hands on her hips, yellow dress fluttering as she tapped a heeled foot like a mother waiting for her toddler to confess that they'd stolen Cheerios from the pantry.

Gabby was not a toddler, nor someone easily impressed by assumed power or any level of condescension from someone who just threw a book into her actual face. From the corner of her eye, she saw Manny get to his feet, his pink pruning shears still in his hand.

"I found this book in my son's room," Rachel said, her voice dripping with venom.

"Oh!" Perhaps Gabby had misunderstood. Of course, any mother would be upset after discovering their child harbored suicidal thoughts. "I'm so sorry that they felt they needed it. They're welcome to keep it if..."

"Keep it?" Rachel's face filled with horror.

No, pious horror. Gabby's instincts crackled. *You're in danger.*

"It is stamped with this, this *library*'s address." The way she said the word library left no doubt as to how much contempt the woman felt for the wooden cupboard. "It discusses a person's sex as though it is something to be questioned. That suggests sexual deviance is okay. As if it were acceptable."

Rachel pretended to gag, her pretty, perfect face contorting into a hate crime. Gabby's mother used to do that as well. She knew exactly who this woman was, confirming her worst nightmare.

Rachel, perhaps sensing that she'd lost Gabby's attention, stepped uncomfortably close. "If your filthy books have infected my child's innocence, their purity, their..." she grasped for the words.

"This book is clearly meant to help teens struggling with thoughts of suicide," Gabby pointed out, finally finding her words. "Please tell me you can see that."

Rachel held up a serious forefinger. "That is between him and God. We have our own books for that, you know."

Gabby did know.

"If you were a mother, you'd understand," Rachel continued.

"I am a mother," Gabby answered.

"Then you understand how this looks." Rachel spread her hands; a fake smile plastered across her teeth.

"Excuse me?" Gabby knew that smile, too. After all, she'd been raised to become this exact woman.

Rachel stepped across to open the door of the tiny library. She pulled out a Sapphic romance, two Regency-era women on the cover. It was one of Ashlin's favorites. Rachel chucked it to the ground. "Filth." A picture book about a rabbit soon followed. An anti-racism board book that made Rachel's eyes bulge. Telling on herself. "Are you one of those groomers, is that it?"

Gabby's brow furrowed. She should do something. She should stop this. The woman had no right to damage the books.

"Books are dangerous." Rachel's voice vibrated with her passion and her eyes filled with righteous tears. She wasn't filled with holy spirit, no matter how much believed she was, it was just simple hate, frothed into furor.

Say something, Gabby. Stand up for the books. Tell her limiting access to books like this causes teen suicides to increase, that people need books like these. But she couldn't summon the words. Couldn't open her mouth.

***

Gabby found herself back in those blue chairs, the old dread sitting on her chest. Three evenings and two mornings every week for seventeen years of her life she'd spent in those chairs, the weave of fabric on the back of the chair in front of her as familiar as the back of her hand. When she was very small, she'd learned that if she relaxed her eyes, let them cross, the weave would pop out into a mesmerizing, three-dimensional pattern.

Her Bible lay open on her hand and her heart fluttered with panic. If she didn't turn to the scripture fast enough, if she couldn't find the book before the preacher started reading, she'd embarrass her parents. But her mind was always wandering, and the pages were so thin.

"Books are dangerous!" The preacher's eyes had the glassy look of a zealot feeding on a captive audience. "They can bring demons into your house. Demons that prey on your children's minds."

Gabby gripped the skeleton key she wore on a friendship bracelet tied around her wrist. The metal warmed to her skin, its pitted iron texture soothing for reasons she never understood. She'd found it, under a tree, which had felt like magic.

And Gabby was a girl who was highly attracted to magic.

Not that she ever let anyone know, of course. She kept it a secret, the same way she kept the burgundy streaks her Bible left on her hand when it got sweaty from holding it secret. Logic stated that her hand-me-down Bible's vinyl cover was disintegrating from the salts in her sweat, but the possibility that she was evil, that her love of magic made her anathema to the scripture, was something young Gabby had wrestled with.

"And for you children," the preacher was saying. Gabby went rigid, as he seemed to speak directly at her. In fact, he gave her a small smile as he met her gaze. "Imagine the humiliation you would heap upon your family if you brought one of those demons into your house. Those books of witchcraft and sin."

Gabby did her best to appear devout and innocent, even as she worked the concept over in her mind. The books they were so worried about, they weren't what the Beholders made them out to be. They weren't as violent or as filled with sex as the Bible she had to read every day. They weren't blasphemous, usually, they didn't fill her brain with clingy demons that made the lights flicker or dishes float out of the cupboards. They were just stories.

Sometimes it seemed like that was the big secret they didn't want her to find out. But if they didn't want her to find out, why did they insist she couldn't attend sex ed classes so that she spent those hours in the library instead? Did they think she wouldn't read the books she was surrounded by? Or had they simply chosen the lesser of two evils: a future woman who understood her sexuality, or one who could read?

***

Gabby dragged herself to the present with a ragged breath. She hadn't let herself go back into those years for a long time. A part of her remained frozen, locked in the trauma she'd earned extricating herself from the cult, getting herself safely excommunicated so she could just live her own life. Losing everything in the process.

That's who Rachel Forrest was, she was Gabby's past, thirty years later, standing on her front lawn, chucking books onto the grass.

Gabby needed to say something, to stand up for herself, for the books. But her head swam with too many thoughts to articulate. *Is your son going to be okay? Oh, gosh, I'm so worried for him. Don't you understand that when someone tells you to be afraid of stories it's because they're trying to control yours? This is private property, who the hell do you think you are?*

"Hey!" shouted Manny. "What do you think you're doing? That's private property!"

Rachel hesitated at that, whether from the warning or a lifetime of church training telling her that she had to obey anything a man said to her. She spread her lips into a thin line and slammed the library door hard enough that the glass cracked. "I want this filth out of my neighborhood!" She stabbed her index finger into the air towards Gabby before storming off, her heels raising a clacketing clamor from the sidewalk.

Even the sound of dress shoes could send Gabby into the past. She closed her eyes for a moment, willing herself to remain in the present. It had been so long since she'd allowed herself to get sucked back into her memories, forgetting this life she'd fought so hard to build. Sure, it wasn't necessarily a particularly impressive life, but it never had to be. It just needed to be hers.

Manny's hand touched Gabby's shoulder, feather light. "Gabs, you okay?" She flinched at his touch despite herself. Manny held up his hands, eyes wide. "It's just me." He knelt to pick up the books from the ground. "She got to you, huh?"

Gabby shook her head, not to disagree, just to clear it. "Yeah, I guess she did."

Manny pursed his lips as he got back to his feet, the books in a stack in his arms. "There's been a lot of weird evangelism happening lately."

Gabby opened the door to the library cupboard carefully, worried the newly cracked window would shatter or worsen. She supposed she could put some duct tape along the crack for now, keep it from getting worse, keep the rain out, and make sure no one got cut. "I've heard people talking about it, but seeing it firsthand was, I don't know... It felt like I step into a time machine that took me to my past."

"There were people picketing Derek's storefront the other day, because of the rainbow sticker in the window," Manny told her. Manny and Derek had been in love for the past three years, though they didn't like to admit it. "They really don't like Trans people."

Gabby watched him carefully. Had something happened that he hadn't told her about? "Then they don't need to know, do they?"

Manny shook his head, eyes on the books as he shelved them one at a time. "I'm glad she's not here to see this." He put his hand over the plaque they'd placed on the side of their library, *For Leona*. "She thought we'd finally entered a golden age where everyone could just be themselves and happy. Safe."

Gabby had thought that, too. When Ashlin told her at four years of age, "I'm going to marry a girl when I grow up," she'd celebrated the girl's freedom, so different from her own childhood. It was only recent events that made Gabby worry she'd set Ashlin up for disappointment.

Retrieving the duct tape from the garage, she remembered something else Leona had told her about. "Did she ever tell you about that magical bookshop she was always chasing down?"

Manny's face lit up. "What did she call it again?"

"The Little Banned Bookshop," Gabby finished, taking a strip of duct tape and sealing the crack on the exterior glass.

Manny leaned on the library, arms crossed. "Didn't it go something like, you get one book or something?"

Gabby grinned. "Yeah. She said the bookshop always moved around, going where it was needed, and if you found it, it would give you this one special book. One that it somehow knew you needed, the one book that could change, or save, your life."

Manny rubbed the plaque affectionately. "It was a good metaphor for LOCKSS."

What? Gabby blinked at Manny. Her hand searched for her old key, the second time today. She'd have to dig it out later. "Locks?"

"It's an acronym for Lots of Copies Keeps Stuff Safe. Basically, the rule that having lots of copies of so-called dangerous books, across private libraries like ours, makes sure they don't disappear. It's magical because the whole community's involved."

Gabby stared at the worn grass in front of the library. She'd taken Leona's story literally. "But…" she started. "Leona said everyone in her old neighborhood collected stories of finding the Bookshop like a dragon hoards coins." She leaned on the library's newly duct-taped door and furrowed her brow at Manny. "Are you sure it wasn't real?"

Manny blinked at her. "A magic bookshop that doesn't obey the laws of physics and just shows up when someone needs it?" His face softened. "Do you want to believe it's real?"

Gabby squirmed. She did. Of course, she did. If something like that existed, there would always be hope, even for girls trapped in their parents' cult like she'd been.

"Hey," Manny asked softly. "Where'd you go?"

"It's just. The worst part of being trapped in a cult like I was, was the feeling that I was alone. That there was no one like me. I couldn't find myself in books. There weren't any to help me understand myself and have as a survival guide for navigating my life. Everything was confusing, because I was always told that things were a certain way, over and over, even though they clearly weren't that way at all. And if I wanted to save myself, I had to ruin my family's reputation, their standing in the church, and abandon them entirely."

Manny shook his head. "But you know that if they're the ones that set that ultimatum, that's on them, not you."

"Yeah, but that's the sort of thing you don't see until you're on the other side of it. But if there was a book, with a character in the same situation, and you found that book, it really could save your life." She shrugged. Maybe she didn't know where she was going with this. Manny knew all of this and more; his experience transitioning was eerily similar to her own journey of becoming her true self. "It would have taken a magic bookshop to get a book like that in my hands back in those days. If I'd heard of one, I would have been just like Leona, wandering the streets all night looking for it."

"That's why people like her," he gestured in the direction Rachel had taken, "are afraid of books."

"Because they can infest your mind with demons," agreed Gabby.

Manny whipped his head around to give her a concerned look. "What?"

Gabby hadn't meant to say that out loud. "Sorry. Something they used to tell me when I was a kid. That books could infest our minds with demons. When what they really meant was, 'we've invested a lot of time brainwashing you and these books could undo all of our hard work.'"

She started walking back to the house with Manny, when something made her turn and glance back at the library. The setting sun bathed its shape in a golden light. "I wanted our library to be that for someone."

"Maybe it already is."

CHAPTER 2

> *Everyone handles adversity differently, and not every-one needs a book from the Little Banned Bookshop. Those who do not require a book can struggle to understand why these books are important to those who do. It might be attractive to argue with these people, but we urge you, instead, to focus on those who do need books.*
>
> *-Care and Feeding of Your Little Banned Bookshop, page 23*

Gabby had hoped she'd never see Rachel Forrest again, but the evangelist had other plans. Within a few days, Gabby spotted Rachel filming the titles in the library cupboard.

Gabby watched from the kitchen window, frozen to the ground, unwilling to believe that this was happening, that Forrest had returned to harass them some more. She wished she had Forrest's audacity, just take out her own phone and start filming her in return, but then what? If she shared the resulting video anywhere, it would just make her friends feel bad about themselves. Why spread despair?

Her fingers fiddled with the skeleton key-she'd found it and started wearing it again-around her wrist. It seemed less tarnished these days than it was when she'd first found it, somehow. At least, from how she remembered it. The comfort, though, that still held. Her fingers, brushing against the squat, silver H of the key's teeth, seemed to be brushing up against hope itself.

Gabby forced herself to stop looking at Rachel, to quell the fierce sense of personal invasion the woman's presence wrought, and focus on the key.

For years after she'd first found the key, she'd wondered what it had opened once upon a time. The older she got, the less she wanted to know. By not knowing, it could open anything. That's what skeleton keys were for right? To open anything at all. Maybe even a cage that you found yourself trapped inside.

Maybe the key was agency. Gabby traced its outline as it pressed into her opposite palm. No. She had agency. She was just too much of a coward to stand up to this woman who clearly represented everything Gabby had escaped, including the angry, bitter Gabby she would have become if she'd been forced to stay in her cage.

***

Gabby, fourteen and feeling very grown up, traveled to the next province over to visit her best friend Lindsay, her husband, and their new baby. Lindsay, who was older than Gabby, invited her to stay for a week. They hadn't seen each other since Lindsay had gotten pregnant and they'd moved so her husband could find better work.

The visit was not as fun as Gabby had hoped. The baby spent most of the time sleeping and Lindsay didn't seem the girl she'd used to be. The husband made Gabby feel uncomfortable, like she had to walk on eggshells. Moreover, they never left the house except for church because he thought it was too cold for the baby. He went out, of course, it was just the womenfolk who were ordered home.

Gabby's parents were an affectionate, loving couple, but this marriage seemed tense. There was something different that Gabby couldn't place until the day came that the baby would not stop crying.

Lindsay shushed, doing a little hopping rhythm on her hips to soothe the baby, over and over, but nothing would help. Her husband glared daggers at her from the couch, turning the tv louder and louder to hear it over the crying. Gabby knew how Lindsay must have felt about that, but Lindsay kept up the pretense of cheery motherhood for the baby's, or maybe Gabby's, sake.

Gabby had a copy of *The Black Stallion* opened, trying desperately to climb inside the story and escape this room. Something was building. It filled the room with a frightening menace. Something was happening, something coiled too tight.

SMACK!

Gabby didn't dare lift her eyes from the book. Some instinct warned her it would make things worse. A tiny, choked voice deep inside of her whispered that Lindsay wouldn't have wanted her to see her husband slap her. Gabby had seen though. She didn't need to look directly at them to see it all play out at the edge of her vision.

"Make that baby shut up!" he screamed, grabbing his coat and walking outside, the door slamming with a swirl of snowflakes as he went.

The baby stopped crying immediately. Lindsay put them in the bassinet and turned down the volume with shaking hands, the violence of his outburst already bruising her cheek. Gabby still sat frozen, staring at the words on the page without blinking. Her hands started sweating through the pages where she gripped the paperback. The paper pilled beneath her thumbs, but she only ground them harder into the book, willing the paper to give. She should have done something. She should have flown to her feet and rushed to her friend's rescue. But how did you protect someone from their husband? He was stronger than both of them. This was his house. Everything she'd ever learned told her she was under his law while she was here.

Now Gabby's hands were shaking, too.

For the first time, Gabby could see the bars of the cage. This was her future. She knew it with the same certainty that she knew winter followed fall. If she didn't get out, then she might as well be dead, because she couldn't bear to waste her life under someone else's fist while she made herself small.

***

Gabby stared at the key. She hadn't become small despite herself, had she? Clearly Rachel Forrest wanted her to be small, wanted to push all the happy people back into their closets so they could be as miserable as she.

Did her husband slap her when her babies cried too much? Was it that trauma that caused her to lash out at books? Maybe he'd beaten her over the book their teenager borrowed and this was the only way for Rachel to get her power back. Gabby sighed and gripped her key tight.

It was another week before the proverbial circus arrived. Manny texted Gabby that she should come home. He'd never done such a thing before, so Gabby didn't hesitate, letting her crew know that she had to go home, some sort of emergency.

"Take the truck, Gabs," said her boss, tossing her the keys. "Just make sure you're back to pick us up before dusk." Some of the newer crew members groaned, but Gabby grinned, knowing exactly what her boss would say about that.

"We've got four months to fit in a year's worth of landscaping, youngsters. If the sun's out, we work." She heard his voice trickle through the air as she reversed the truck, Mulvaney Landscaping Co. emblazoned proudly on the side.

Gabby geared down as she pulled onto her street and saw a small crowd gathered about the Little Free Library.

"What's going on?" she murmured. Then she noticed the crowd itself, entirely female, all of them perfectly coiffed, in dresses and dress shoes.

They held up picket signs as Gabby crawled past, unable to keep herself from reading them. *Groomer Library. Pornography is NOT for kids. Library of FILTH. Save the children!* They were all done with black sharpie on neon Bristol board.

Did y'all have a full-on craft night to make these? Gabby wondered.

She would have liked to keep on driving past, but Manny wouldn't have texted unless he felt unsafe. Besides, Gabby was the one Rachel had her sights on, not Manny, and Gabby didn't want that to change.

Gasps of horror rose from the picketers as Gabby pulled into the driveway. Someone took a picture of her as she got out of the truck, which made Gabby roll her eyes. She worked in the dirt, beautifying neighborhoods for people just like them, she didn't have the luxury of staying clean all day and never breaking a sweat. Gabby reached for her water bottle and went into the house.

Inside the dark space of the entryway, Gabby peeled off her work gloves to clutch the skeleton key. "Here is the hope you need," the key seemed to promise, and she believed it. She leaned against the shut door and closed her eyes, giving herself a moment to collect herself.

"Manny?" she called.

"Oh, thank god," he said, coming around the corner with a vase held defensively in his hands. "I thought they'd broken in."

"No." They wouldn't do that, would they? "Are you okay?"

"They had a news van out there, Gabby. They were being interviewed." He knuckled his mouth. "This is bad. This is getting bad. Our house will be on the news."

This made no sense, but she hated how close to a panic attack Manny had become. "Does anyone even watch the news anymore?"

"They do if it's a video on social media."

A sliver of dread cooled her heart. No, she couldn't focus on that right now. "Okay, what do you need to do to feel safe right now? Want me to book us a hotel for the night?" she asked.

Manny's shoulders released a barely imperceptible bit of tension. "No, I don't think we need to do that. I just got...I don't want to be alone in here while they're out there feeding off of hate crimes on our lawn."

Troubled, Gabby cast a glance to the front window. "Who are those people? They're not our neighbors."

Oh no, she realized all at once. What if that was Rachel's church group? If their library became a pet project… "We're not actually doing anything wrong, right? People are legally allowed to give away books?" They had to register their library to a national record when they opened it twelve years ago, got an assigned number and a listing in the directory and everything. The library cupboards were encouraged and welcomed to neighborhoods because they promoted literacy.

Manny crossed his arms, chewing on his thumbnail. "You mean since the world went nuts and the book burning fascists got real loud? It *used* to be fine."

Gabby frowned. "You don't feel safe, Manny. Do you want me to take it down?"

"I don't want the bad guys to win," he insisted.

Gabby wasn't convinced, but Manny usually took a bit longer than everyone else to sit with his feelings and understand himself. Trauma did that to a person. "Okay. If you change your mind, let me know."

"What happens to the kids if we take it down?" His voice cracked as he said it.

Gabby clutched at her key. Maybe it was silly of them to think their library could make a difference. Naive, or something. It was their version of Leona's Banned Bookshop. Maybe it didn't have magical abilities, couldn't move through space and know exactly what book someone needed, but it was better than nothing. A sob built in her chest and tears slipped down her cheeks right on cue.

Manny cocked his head, giving her an upside-down smile. "What would Leona do?"

Gabby let out a noise somewhere between a giggle and a sob. "My god, did I ever tell you? My mother used to try and convert her, for years. Obviously, I have weird feelings about the memories that drags up, but that's how I first met Leona."

Manny leveled his gaze, his fingers spread out, jazz-style, in front of him. "Excuse me, *what*?"

"Manny, it was amazing. She would toss her wig on the porch post and walk down the front steps of her trailer like a movie star. She still smoked then, with one of those long white cigarette holders that were a special kind of fabulous even then. She'd be in a lace teddy, her chest hair out and proud, this silk dressing gown slipping off her shoulder. There were these fuzzy, heeled slippers, I'd never seen them anywhere but on Miss Piggy, and Leona would just settle into her lawn furniture and let my mother preach away."

Manny nodded, his brow furrowed. "Why?"

Gabby shook her head. "I don't know. Maybe she sensed that my mom just wanted someone to listen to her for once. Maybe Leona took a perverse pleasure in watching

this woman who condemned her lifestyle squirm."
Gabby frowned. Leona had always paid for the literature her mother brought, despite all evidence suggest-
ing she was desperately poor. Why had she done that?

"Maybe it was for you," suggested Manny. "Maybe
Leona was worried about you. How old were you
then?"

No, that didn't sit right. "Six, maybe eight? One day
we went back and her trailer wasn't there anymore."
She'd worried about Leona, back then. She'd never seen
a whole home disappear without a trace, leaving nothing more than an indent in the dirt. When Gabby ran
into her again, decades later, at Ashlin's first Pride pa-
rade, Gabby had struggled to reconcile the worlds that
smashed together to make that happen.

"This is the wildest story I've never heard. I can't
believe you never told me this before!"

"Sorry. It's hard to dredge up the religious memories,
I can get kind of stuck in them. But since the picketing
few are out there, it feels like I'm in there anyway."

"Did she recognize you?" He screwed up his mouth.
"No, she couldn't have, could she?"

Gabby shook her head. "Leona looked the same, but I'd
gone from prim Jesus kid to a full-blown Mom. I think,
when she learned my story, she might have suspected. And

I probably look more like my mom than I'm willing to admit to myself."

"And you always hate telling your story," Manny pointed out.

Gabby shrugged. She did. People viewed her differently afterward. Growing up in a cult sounds fascinating, until people found out it was one of those aggressively proselytizing, "bible-thumper" cults that tended to give the sort of person Gabby found herself attracted to "the ick." Heck, thinking about those days gave her the ick.

"We talked about it eventually," Gabby told him. "I apologized to her, which of course she refused to hear."

"Maybe she thought you were a baby Queer," teased Manny.

No, that wasn't it. Leona was focused on her mom the whole time, not Gabby, but Gabby didn't correct him. She jingled her truck keys. "I have to go back to work eventually. You're welcome to come with, or I can drop you off at Derek's."

Manny sighed and took a final peer out the window. "I wish I had the balls to put on some fancy lingerie, coif my chest hair, and go be fabulous at them."

Gabby giggled at the image. "I'm not sure you could pull that off."

The library drama wasn't over that night, or the next. Rachel's reels went viral on the outrage circuit, the protests continued, and the attention grew unbearable.

Neither Manny Nor Gabby wanted to give in, to let this neighborhood dictator take away their chance to make the world a better place. But Manny started breaking out in hives and spent more and more nights at Derek's apartment. The stress was clawing at Gabby too, nightmares she thought she'd left behind forever were back, and more than once she'd awoken screaming from a dream that she was caged. Iron bars placed over her bed so she couldn't sit up, just grip them and scream.

Worse, a wriggling, toxic sense of shame had returned to the bottom of her soul. The key's comfort couldn't touch that. She'd grown up with that shame, telling her she was all wrong, on the wrong side of history, the wrong side of heaven, the right side of hell. That the demons had infested her soul so deep that free will was just a concept of the damned.

"Mom, I'm worried about you." Ashlin held both of Gabby's hands, the mirror of her brown eyes wide and troubled.

"I can take it." Gabby squeezed Ashlin's hands. "Better our Little Free Library than the municipal one, right?"

Ashlin's freckled face clouded over.

"Oh, no. What's happened?"

"They're petitioning the libraries, too." Ashlin sighed, tucking her shoulder-length brown hair behind her ears with both hands. "And the youth club is worried about losing our funding because of our open solidarity policy." She held up her hands. "We'll find new funding if we need to, mind, but you need to understand. It's not great out there."

Gabby got up suddenly, putting her coffee cup in the sink and scrubbing it just to hear the white noise of the faucet. "I hate this. We can't let this happen."

"Mom." Ashlin's voice took on a steadiness that Gabby had always admired. "What we need to do right now is strengthen our communities. We need to be there for each other and keep each other safe." She narrowed her eyes at her mother. "We don't need to burn ourselves out on the first battle when the war is only beginning."

"A war! I'm too tired for wars." Gabby hated herself for complaining, but she meant it, to the marrow of her bones. "Wars are for twenty-year-olds who are still powered by leftover teenage rebellion. I want to know that my daughter's safe."

Ashlin chuckled and crossed her arms over her black t-shirt. "Mom, I know how to keep myself safe. You taught me well. And I'm safer than you are right now."

Gabby closed her eyes. Ashlin was right, but, "Everyone sees those viral newscasts, not just the book banners. Their kids see them. Other kids who never heard of half of these books, they're discovering them too. And every morning, there are fewer books in the cupboard because they're coming out, when they feel safe, to get the books they need." Gabby spread her hands. "How do I take it down, knowing that?"

Ashlin exhaled heavily, deliberating this new information. She didn't have an answer, either.

In the end, the choice was removed altogether when their landlord stepped in. "I can't lie, Miss Gabby, I'm getting a little worried that my property is in danger with all of this protest goings-on."

Gabby stared, her mouth dry, unable to speak. "But, we have a lease."

"Well, I had my lawyer look at the terms of the lease and the hubbub you've been causing has nullified your end of the bargain." He gave her a greasy smile that let her know he was lying. "Besides, my own dear mother is ailing and needs a place of her own."

Gabby stared down the street. She'd read enough shady-landlord reddit threads to know that claiming familial need was a popular tactic among the less-reputable landlords. She just hadn't realized that her landlord was one of those.

"You've got one week to take down the library causing the problems. You do that on time, and I'll give you three months to find a new place instead of two."

Three months was nothing during the current housing crisis. Gabby stared at the notice in her hand. They could fight it, they might have some legal ground, but everything about this place had gotten irrevocably tainted of late. Did she really want to fight another battle to keep living down the street from a monster who already had Gabby in her sights? Gabby just needed to get used to the idea, then she'd figure out something for herself, too. She had a good, steady job. She'd be okay. Her world was not collapsing around her.

Of course, those thoughts did little to stem the sobs that threatened to unleash themselves on her front steps in full view of Rachel Forrest and her picket brigade.

They waited for Sunday, when all the protestors were stowed in their churches, to take down the library in peace. Neither Manny nor Gabby could bear to do it under their gloating gaze.

They'd decided to donate the books to Ashlin's youth center, where they still might do some good. Manny solemnly piled the books into reusable shopping bags while Gabby averted her eyes, wishing she didn't feel like she'd failed the books.

Once empty, Gabby unscrewed the cupboard from the fence post that held it up and carried it into the garage. Ashlin and Manny dug up the concrete brace they'd poured for the fence post. When Gabby returned, it lay on its side, a dirty time capsule beside an empty hole.

"I was fourteen when we poured this thing," Ashlin remarked. She reached over, taking first Gabby's hand, then Manny's with her other. "This isn't a funeral. This is something outside of our control that does not break us."

Manny released a dramatic sigh. "I thought we agreed that I got to say the wise, clever thing this time. Nobody ever lets the man have the moment anymore." His mouth quirked as he tried to hold back his laugh.

"And thank you for breaking the tension, Uncle Manny," said Ashlin in a fake-exasperated tone.

"That's why we keep him around," added Gabby. She smiled despite herself. The three of them slipped so easily back into their old dynamic. Her mood brightened and her heart filled with love for her makeshift family.

"Oh! I almost forgot!" Ashlin jogged to her car, a rusty hatchback that made Gabby nervous, and opened the trunk. She pulled out a potted cedar bush from its depths with a big grin.

"I told you that we have to move, right?" asked Gabby, hoping Ashlin hadn't spent too much on the tree.

"I know." Ashlinn wriggled the tree from its pot. "But it's a cedar tree."

Gabby exchanged glances with Manny. "So?"

"So, cedar trees are known to repel pests." She planted the tree in the empty post hole with a flourish and grinned up at them both.

Gabby shook her head. Gods, she loved this girl.

"I'll help you put the books in your car," offered Manny.

Gabby grabbed the abandoned pot and went into the garage to get a bucket of water for the new tree. She stopped when she noticed a book inside the dismantled library cupboard. An unfamiliar, purple-covered book sat on the top shelf. Frowning, Gabby opened the door to retrieve it and send it along with Ashlin, but she froze when she read the title, *Care and Feeding of Your Little Banned Bookshop.*

Chapter 3

> *Little Banned Bookshops do not exist in every town, but there are libraries, and online bookstores. Shopkeepers are encouraged to take advantage of these places to reach those in need that the Bookshop itself cannot reach. Creativity is encouraged. Teamwork with your Bookshop is essential.*
>
> *-Care and Feeding of Your Little Banned Bookshop, page 105*

Gabby turned the book over in her hands. *Care and Feeding of Your Little Banned Bookshop.* She half-expected to see Leona's name behind the front cover. She chided herself for the magical thinking it brought out in her. It was just a book, after all; it didn't mean that magical book-shops exist. Manny probably had the rights of that, but it had been a hopeless sort of morning thus far and she wanted to believe it was real, to believe that somewhere, books were out of the Rachel Forrests of the world's reach.

Gabby hugged the book to her chest, her old key clunking against the back cover, and closed her eyes. "Thank you," she said out loud, to no one in particular.

Once Ashlin had gone home, Gabby opened the book while propped up in her bed, the soft light of her bedside lamp creating a sphere of calm the outside world could not breach. Toebeans Morrison, the tuxedo cat she'd rescued years ago, purred contentedly at her side, no doubt grateful she'd finally stopped anxiety cleaning everything in the house.

Gabby opened the book to the first page.

Of all stories written and told, of all books banned and hidden away, the story of this Bookshop had hoped you would find it. You have been trusted with these pages, the lifeblood of the Little Banned Bookshop, and should consider yourself honored indeed. Read on, friend, for these words are meant for you.

Goosebumps lifted the hair on her arms and Gabby smiled to herself. Yes, this was exactly the book she needed to escape reality for a while. She settled in to read.

A few passages made her frown, for it seemed the author stuck a little too close to the idea that this book was an actual care guide for what Gabby could only describe as a living bookshop.

The Bookshop is innocent of all political machinations. They are simply driven to the preservation of all banned books. Because of this, the Bookshop would happily give out any book to any petitioner, without thought of self-preservation. This has led to the endangerment of many a Bookshop simply because said Bookshop is not capable of differentiating between a copy of Anne Frank: the Diary of a Young Girl *and* How to Censor and Shut Down Little Banned Bookshops. *Despite their innocence, the Bookshop is quite capable of regret, guilt, and prone to depression in scenarios where it has dispensed a book which has brought harm to others.*

This is why a Shopkeeper is needed for every Bookshop. The Shopkeeper's main duty is to protect and nurture their Little Banned Bookshop. Once the shop and Shopkeeper have bonded, the Bookshop will rely upon the Shopkeeper to advise them of when it is safe to give a patron their book and when it is wiser to withhold. Please be aware that these withholding occasions tend to be far and few between.

Gabby sighed. What kind of book was this? It took itself so seriously that it didn't read to her like fiction at all. *What if it's not?* The question made her pulse quicken.

Knock! Knock! Knock!

Toebeans Morrison's purring ceased and his ears twitched in annoyance at the sound, "Was that someone at the door?" Gabby asked him, getting out of bed and reaching for a bra.

Knock! Knock! Knock!

It was coming from the patio door off the kitchen. Gabby hesitated. It was late, she wasn't expecting anyone, and Manny was at Derek's. Still, she sensed an urgency behind the knock that compelled her to answer.

She made her way to the kitchen in darkness, until she spied the shape of a teenager in a hoodie on the deck. They held up a hand and waved. *Good gods, Gabby, have you no sense of self-preservation,* she thought to herself as she flicked on the light and opened the sliding door.

The teenager hugged their arms to their chest. "I'm sorry to bother you so late." Their eyes looked desperate, wide, belying the fireflies wisping in the background behind them.

Gabby's mothering instincts kicked in. She opened the door wider, "Would you like to come in?"

The kid nodded, giving a furtive glance to the side before stepping into the kitchen. They didn't sit down, choosing instead to stand, crossing and uncrossing their arms.

"Are you in any danger? Is there someone I can call for you?"

They shook their head. "No. Thank you. It's just..." They stopped talking, wringing their hands.

Gabby filled the kettle, turned it on, and reached for two mugs. She had to do something. It was too awkward to just stand there in her mushroom print pajamas waiting for this youngster to say whatever was on their mind, which seemed like a considerable something. It was too late for coffee and tea seemed wrong, so she settled on spooning hot chocolate into the mugs. "Take your time. This is a safe place."

Gabby's guest was still gathering their words when Gabby sat down at the table with her mug, setting the other opposite her. "I'm Gabby. My pronouns are she and her. You can sit down if you like." It came out awkward, but somehow that suited the moment.

To her relief, they sat. "My pronouns are they and them." Their hands trembled as they reached for the hot chocolate, stopped, and pulled them back into their lap. "I don't deserve you being so nice to me."

Something in their voice tugged at Gabby's heart. "I don't know about that, but if you'd like to explain, I'll listen."

"No. Apologize. I came to apologize. My name is Ronnie. Forrest." They flicked their brown eyes up to watch her reaction.

Gabby sipped her hot chocolate as she put the pieces together. "Your mom found the book you got from our Little Free Library."

"I didn't mean to leave it where she could find it, honest I didn't. She just found it." The words spilled quickly now they were coming. "She gets so focused on things and she takes things so far. And tonight, I was coming home and saw that the books were gone and I'm just so sorry." They smacked at an escaped tear with their hand.

"Ronnie. You're not responsible for other people's actions, even if they're your mom. This is not something you should feel guilty for."

Their hands hugged their mug now. "But you had to take it down?"

Gabby sighed. "Yes, unfortunately we rent this place, we don't own it, and our landlord pulled his weight in that respect." She purposefully left out the rest of the story.

"That sucks. All those books." Their shoulders sagged.

"My daughter works at the youth center on Tenth Street, so we were able to donate the books to them. They're open every day from nine to nine if you ever happen to be in that area."

Ronnie nodded slowly, absorbing that information. "Will that book be there? The *Cruel World* one?"

Gabby had forgotten about the backup copies she and Manny had kept in the cupboard over the fridge until now. She could just give them one.

A part of her hesitated. What if Rachel Forrest had sent them here, setting her up for just this scenario and whatever twisted thrill the woman got from making Gabby's life difficult. She'd let a minor into her house, alone, with no further witnesses beyond Toebeans Morrison. Gabby could get into a lot of trouble for this.

Or she could save this kid's life.

A silly thought bubbled up from the back of her mind. *Be the magic bookshop you want to see in the world.*

Gabby dragged her chair to the fridge and stood on it, opening the cupboard. Sure enough, a stack of black and white books waited for her. *Hello Cruel World: 101 Alternatives to Suicide for Teens, Freaks, and other Outlaws.* She opened the front cover of the topmost book, relieved to see that it wasn't stamped with their library's mark. Books could come from anywhere, after all.

Ronnie's face brightened when they saw what she held, but Gabby didn't hand it over right away. Instead, she went to a drawer and pulled out a large zipper freezer bag. "If you keep the book inside one of these, you have more options for hiding it. Under a bush, in the hollow of a tree." Her mind went immediately to the day she found her skeleton key, hidden in the dirt. "Somewhere your mom won't find it."

"Are you sure? I mean, after those videos my mom made?" asked Ronnie, looking longingly at the book but not taking it.

"I am sure. You staying alive and thriving is more important to me than whatever a bunch of strangers online think of me."

Ronnie blinked with enough surprise that Gabby had to fight the urge to hug them. "Really?" they asked.

"Of course."

Ronnie took a step toward her and stopped. "May I – may I hug you?"

"Okay." They rushed into her arms, their shoulders shuddering with silent sobs. Gabby held them tighter. She knew exactly how much practice it took to cry that hard in silence, though she hadn't remembered that in years.

When Ronnie finally released her, they swiped the evidence of their tears away quickly and tucked the book into the freezer bag.

"My daughter's name is Ashlin. The one that works at the youth center. You can trust her, if you need to. Please promise me you'll go there if things get too bad."

Ronnie sniffled, tucking the bagged book up under their shirt. "I'll try. Thanks for everything, Gabby."

She watched as they slipped out the back door. The fireflies twinkled as she drew the door shut. The key around her wrist seemed strangely warm as it bounced against her skin. For a moment, she thought it had an orange glow, but surely that was just a trick of the light.

Work soon shifted into high gear, Mulvaney's Landscaping racing against the season. A few new students joined the crew and days stretched from dawn to dusk. It was good, hard work. The sunshine and exercise lifted Gabby's spirits as it did every year, and she fell into bed so tired at the end of the day she didn't have time to dwell on the past or Rachel Forrest. Sleep became a blissful oblivion. *Care and Feeding of Your Little Banned Bookshop* rested on Gabby's night table, waiting for her to have the time to read further.

The moment finally presented itself one evening when the rain sent the landscaping crews home early. Gabby sat on the ragged, comfy chair that, when it rained, smelled like a dog they didn't have. Manny insisted on draping a sheet over the thing when they had guests, but they both knew it was the best chair in the house. Neither of them told their guests they'd found it on the side of the road with a handwritten "free" sign on it while Ashlin was in grade school. Gabby could still picture little Ashlin curled up in the chair, half its size, doing her homework.

She cracked open *Care and Feeding*, embarrassed to discover that she hadn't made it through the first chapter. Section. Whichever it was. She missed having enough time to read a book in a day.

"Gabs, you're home!" Manny stood in the entryway to the kitchen, looking worried.

She closed the book, putting it face down in her lap. "Yeah, finally rained. You okay? You seem worried about something."

He ran his fingers through his hair and sat on the couch with a small huff. "I've been needing to talk to you about what we're going to do now that we have to move."

A small pang of guilt shot through Gabby's gut. She had absolutely been putting this off until work calmed down and hadn't even considered how that might cause Manny anxiety. "Sorry, I didn't mean to drop the ball there. I mean, we have almost two months, right? Seems like plenty of time, but if you're stressing, I'll go along with whatever you find."

Manny winced. "That's actually what I wanted to talk to you about."

Gabby sat up straighter. She'd clearly missed something.

Manny took a deep breath. "Derek asked me to move in with him."

Gabby blinked, absorbing what this meant. Manny would be living with Derek, not with her. But Manny and Gabby had been house mates for over a decade. They were family. At the same time, this was a momentous step in his relationship with Derek. "Wow, you must be thrilled," she said, her voice sounding strange to her ears.

Manny gave her an excited grin as he nodded, his eyes shining. "Right? I know it's a huge commitment, but I think we're ready. And we've kind of been talking about getting married next summer." He held up his hand. "Nothing's set in stone, not yet. Just thinking, but..." His eyes were fever bright. "I'm really happy."

Gabby smiled, swallowing back a lump in her throat. He *was* happy, that was clear. So why did it feel like she was losing her best friend? Would their easy friendship be the same if they weren't tripping over each other all the time?

"And I want you and Ashlin to come over for dinner at least every other Sunday," Manny went on.

Gabby folded her hands in her lap to hide their shaking. This was just trauma coming out, she assured herself. Sure, this was the end of an era, but it didn't need to be cataclysmic. She gripped her key so tight her hands ached, though that could have just been from the rain.

***

Gabby sat in the woven blue chairs for the last time, willing all of this to be over. Her father insisted she be here, to "endure the shame you brought upon this family."

She closed her eyes. She'd set everything up like dominoes. All her life they'd told her exactly what she needed to do to get herself excommunicated; everything they despised in non-Beholders. Each one a domino that could break her out of her cage. Then, when she had been ready, she took a deep breath and pushed the first domino.

It had worked, perhaps too well. Everyone always seemed so eager to believe the worst of someone once they believed the demons got a hold of them. And Gabby had always been a bookish girl.

The reality of what she'd done was beginning to trickle through her desperate need to break free. To not end up like Lindsay. Gabby knew no one outside of the cult besides a few schoolteachers and classmates; Beholders were not allowed to fraternize with non-Beholders. She'd be on her own.

The preacher shuffled to the podium, his face a careful study of sorrow and betrayal. "We have an unfortunate announcement this evening. Gabrielle Marchand has been excommunicated. As per our sacred scripture, she is to be expelled from our community. From this point on, she is as one dead to us. No one may speak to her without fear of divine retribution."

Gabby stared at the weave, crossing her eyes for the last time, the key clutched so tight in her fist the indent would last for hours.

"Remember, my Beholder brethren. We do this out of love, so that Gabrielle understands what a loving, peaceful community she has lost. We do this to beget the loneliness and regret necessary to send her running back into our Savior's arms."

Gabby wondered what would happen if she threw up right there on the church carpet. What story would they spin that into once she was gone. Guilt. The demons trying to escape. She clenched the key tighter. She had a plan. She'd packed everything she could into her hiking knapsack. Her journals, her favorite stuffie, some clothes. They would be the only memories of her childhood. She'd wanted some photos, but her mother had said no.

Gabby's father let out a horrible howl, sobbing into his hands. She watched from the far side of her stoic, clenched jaw mother, with an unexpected sense of detachment. She had done the worst thing a daughter could do in his eyes; she'd refused the life he'd chosen for her. She'd tried to explain that it didn't fit, but he couldn't hear over all the religious noise he'd been fed all these years.

Soon. This would be over soon.

She wasn't allowed back in the house, but she had all her camping gear ready and she knew a spot, deep in the woods, where she'd be safe. At least until it got cold. But she still had a few months to figure all of that out.

Finally, the meeting ended, and everyone stood. Gabby moved for the door, desperate to escape the confines of the place, when her mother gripped her arm above her wrist. "How could you do this to us?" her mother hissed under her breath.

✳✳✳

"Hey." Manny touched Gabby's hand, bringing her back to the present. "Are you okay with all of this? You just got really quiet."

Gabby's cheeks warmed. "Yeah. I'm thrilled for you. It's just... the end of an era, you know?"

He nodded. "It is. And I am aware that there's a housing crisis happening, so if you need help, I'm your guy."

A spark of panic fizzled in her chest. Would she be able to afford a place on her own? Her job was seasonal, how would that look to a potential new landlord? Maybe she could find a new roommate, put out some feelers.

"It is nice that something good came of all that evangelist nonsense," Manny added.

Gabby reached for the book before she realized that he meant his relationship. "Yeah."

"You know they're still reposting the same videos, trying to keep everyone riled up?" said Manny. "Calling us groomers and all sorts of awful things. It's probably a good thing we're leaving with neighbors like that."

"I don't get the groomer thing at all. I mean, I've heard it used that way in other evangelical smear campaigns. Usually against Drag Queen Storytimes at the library."

Manny sighed. "Yeah, they're weirdly obsessed with those." He rolled his eyes. "Can't have children exposed to *Mrs. Doubtfire.* "

Gabby shook her head. "I met so many groomers growing up and they all had positions of esteem in the church." She cringed at the memories. "These older, unmarried men who would corner me and assure me that they'd wait for me until I grew up. I guess it's probably a product of a very small dating pool, but it always made my guts hurt." She left out the part where the church also trained her to feel guilty for her reaction. And at fault.

Manny stared at her, brow furrowed. "Seriously? How old were you?"

"I don't know, maybe eleven when it started?"

He looked so horrified that Gabby wished she hadn't said anything. She pulled out the book to change the subject. "Hey, look at this book I found."

"*Care and Feeding of Your Little Banned Bookshop,*" he read aloud, not reaching for it. His eyes lit up with recognition. He really did seem to have a lightbulb inside him lately. "Wait, that's what Leona called her magic bookstore, didn't she?"

"Yeah. I found it the day we took down the library."

His eyes flicked up to meet hers, not voicing the question of why she didn't share it then. "So, what is it, exactly? Like a manual on how to feed a bookstore?" He made a face. "That's a bit weird, no?"

She tried to quell the defensiveness his words ignited in her. "I haven't actually gotten to the feeding part yet."

Manny chuckled. "Well, I would read that first. Make sure you don't end up in some *Little Shop of Horrors* situation."

Gabby shot him a wary look, but he was already on his tangent. "Feed me, Gabby! Feed me all your fascists until your city is safe!" He warmed to his theatrics and smacked his lips. "Mmm... fascists are delicious. There's nothing like stewing in hate to season the meat just so."

Gabby laughed despite herself, tossing a pillow at him.

Later that night, once she was alone, she took out the book and checked the table of contents for the feeding section, just in case.

Little Banned Bookshops thrive on energy. Of course, their favorite is the energy they get giving a petitioner their book, but it's best to consider this a dessert energy.

Over the long term, the healthiest sustenance a Bookshop can receive is the energy most of us give off by simply reading. As you can imagine, genre is irrelevant, though it does help if the reader is enjoying the book. Most Bookshop keepers should aim to read a minimum of two hours a day to maintain a robust bookstore.

CHAPTER 4

Historically, new Shopkeepers discover their Bookshops during times of upheaval. This may be political upheaval, cultural upheaval, and/or personal upheaval. We understand that this can be overwhelming, confusing, and possibly even traumatic for future Shopkeepers who may not fully understand what is happening, but please believe us, your fellow Banned Bookshop keepers, that your Little Banned Bookshop will take as much care of you as you do of it.

- Care and Feeding of Your Little Banned Bookshop, p. 36.

Gabby groaned, her body aching from another day of laying sod. Not her favorite task, but certainly the one with the most dramatic results, even if it left her stiff.

She shuffled into the kitchen to make coffee when her phone trilled a notification. Gabby clicked the kettle on and opened her phone to see a message from Manny.

"Did you see this?" The linked video opened automatically.

Gabby squinted in disbelief to see her work truck in the video. She watched herself get out of the truck and glance over to the camera, when the video cut to Rachel Forrest. Her make up was immaculate, every hair perfectly in place.

"I didn't notice this right away, but there is a business logo on that truck. To one Mulvaney Landscaping. I did some research and it turns out that they are a major local landscaping company."

The video zoomed into her face. "Does Mulvaney Landscaping take care of your landscaping needs?"

Rachel looked off into the distance, and when she returned her gaze to the camera, her eyes were filled with tears. "They hire teenagers to work with them, as a summer job. Teenagers, exposed to that established groomer, Gabrielle Marchand."

Gabby sucked in her breath, her chest tight, as a fizz of cold panic raced through her body. They knew her name. They knew where she worked. Doxxed, that was the term, wasn't it? A sudden fury chased the panic from her thoughts. If they doxxed Manny like this, there would be hell to pay.

The video cut to a still of the old Little Free Library, sending a stab of longing through Gabby's heart. The picture focused on the titles, everyone of them like an old friend, but in Rachel's video a threatening song played over them. "I won't let her infect the hardworking children of this town like she infected my beloved son." Rachel's voice trembled with emotion.

A wave of disgust rolled through Gabby. She shouldn't be surprised, but hearing the woman publicly misgender her kid was too much.

Rachel held up a phone number written in red sharpie on a piece of white paper. Gabby recognized it as the Mulvaney Landscaping office number with a spreading sense of detachment. She should stop watching, she should turn the phone off right now jand do whatever it took to salvage her day off. But she couldn't summon the movement required to turn this thing off, so it played on.

"We're going to save those kids. For Jesus! If you've hired Mulvaney Landscaping, call them and tell them you don't want this groomer near your flower beds. And I need every one of you to pick up the phone and call to demand they fire her immediately before any more children are infected with her gay agenda."

The horror in Rachel's voice as she ground out "gay agenda" might have been something Gabby and Manny laughed at once upon a time, but Gabby didn't feel laughing today. She set her phone down and went back to bed, pulling the blankets over her head and shutting out the world.

She couldn't say how long she stayed before the phone rang. Gabby checked the caller ID, hoping it wasn't her boss. Ashlin.

"Mom? Are you okay? Manny sent me the video." There was a long pause that Gabby thought she should have filled, but she couldn't think of anything to say. "I've done some research on what to do if you're doxxed for work, so I need you to trust me. You need to deactivate all of your social media profiles ASAP. Mom? Are you listening?"

"I'm listening," Gabby answered. She wanted to be far, far away from all of this. She wanted to go back to her easy, cheerful life before she ever met Rachel Forrest.

"They had your full name on there, Mom. They're going to find you and start sending you terrible messages that are going to seriously affect your mental health. The sooner you shut your profiles down, the better for you. Don't respond to them, don't engage, just sit tight."

"At least I'm good at doing that," Gabby murmured, and immediately regretted it. She was slipping into a dark hole. It was all happening again. She could feel the strength and resilience she'd worked so hard to build for herself draining away, leaving only the low self-esteem and shattered confidence of her youth. She didn't want Ashlin to see this. Didn't want anyone to see this *Snap out of it, Gabby*. As if it were that easy. "Sure, sweetie, I can do that. And I'll deactivate everything as soon as I'm off my phone."

"Good." Ashlin's voice didn't sound relieved. "Please do that now and call me back when you're done."

The phone went quiet as Ashlin hung up without waiting for a response. Gabby forced herself to sit up and open her social media icons, along with a few webpages on how to deactivate them all. Would a month be long enough? Two? Gabby blinked back unwelcome tears. She'd be living somewhere else by then. A completely different life she couldn't see from here.

The idea unsettled her almost as much as the overwhelming number of notifications she had on her profiles. Ashlin was right, they'd definitely found her. Now that the Little Free Library was gone, she was their new pet project.

There was one site, unlinked from the others, where she hadn't used her name as her username. Heck, she was hardly on there. That one, at least, remained quiet. Maybe she'd keep that one active for a little while longer, just to feel like she was still a person in the world.

Before she closed her other accounts, she checked Manny's profile quickly. Nothing out of the ordinary. He was safe, for now. She'd ask Ashlin when she called her back if they should suggest he lock his accounts down too, before they found him.

Her fingers ached from gripping the steering wheel too tight on the drive to work and Gabby couldn't seem to bring herself to open the car door. Until she went inside, everything was still just a series of frustrating events in her personal life. Once she went in there, that could change.

She never wore the key to work. Jewelry was prohibited and she'd hate to lose it trimming some stranger's overgrown hedge, but she missed its comfort today.

"Okay, let's do this," she said aloud. She'd faced worse than this.

She'd always enjoyed the smell of fuel, mown lawn, and earth that filled the shop. The staff gathered in a circle of chairs, old-timers smoking, everyone with a cup of coffee in their hands, chatting about their lives.

It was hard to miss the worried looks, the few clenched jaws, and one or two bright eyes that followed her in. Talon seemed genuinely happy to see her, lifting his hand in a wave.

Gabby tried to smile back, but her butterflies were overwhelming her. She could feel her old self-esteem issues waiting, stalking, ready to pounce, just below the surface of her thoughts. Should she pretend like nothing happened, sit in her usual chair and fake the big belly laughs that once came so easily?

"Gabby, I need to see you in my office," Bryce rarely came out of his office this time of day. There was no way this was about anything but Rachel's anti-Gabby campaign.

She followed him inside with a sense of dread and sat down in the worn black chair where she'd sat for over a decade, discussing the upcoming season. Did any of that matter anymore? The smell of years-old tobacco smoke clung to the walls, waning and waxing with the day's humidity. She'd never noticed just how shabby this room had grown before, the scuffed walls, the drooping ceiling tiles.

"I suppose you know why you're here," Bryce began. He had always been a friendly, twinkly eyed man, but in this moment, he reminded her of the Beholders preachers, gearing up to list her wrongdoings and berate her for making the cult look like less than perfection. Her chest tightened, her guts curdled, and twenty-five years of freedom disappeared until she was that little girl again.

"We've had these nutsoes calling us nonstop, threatening to picket the office because we're protecting a groomer." He held up his hand. "Talon actually set me straight on what that means and how they're using it, so to be clear, I don't think you're what they say you are, but good god Gabby, how did you get mixed up with these people?"

Gabby sent a silent thank you to Talon for standing up for her. Kid couldn't lay sod to save his life, but she loved him for this. He'd always be welcome on her crew.

Bryce was looking at her like he expected an answer. "That woman who makes the videos just moved into my neighborhood and has it out for me." She should elaborate, but something stopped her. Bryce had worked with Gabby for fifteen years. He knew her. She shouldn't have to defend herself just because a group of self-righteous bigots targeted her.

"I'm caught between a rock and a hard place here, Gabby. The business can't lose a season to these Bible thumpers. We've got twenty-eight staff here who have their own bills to pay and I've already had six clients threaten to cancel if I don't cut you loose." He raked his hands through his thinning hair. "This is absolutely nuts." He dropped heavily into the chair across from her. "I swear to god, Gabby, I'll hire you back next season after all this blows over, no loss in seniority."

Best not swear to god on my account, she thought, bracing herself for the inevitable expectation of comforting him for needing to fire her. After fifteen years of busting her butt for his company.

He leaned forward and pointed a finger at her. "And this is a lay-off, understood? I'm not firing you. You'll still be able to collect your unemployment benefits."

A hundred details he should know about her crew's project surfaced in her mind, ready on her tongue, but she bit them back. Fifteen years. "Any severance pay?"

Bryce winced. "With these cancellations, Gabs, I'm hurting."

But he'd said they'd only threatened to cancel, if he didn't fire her. A small, cold chill entered her veins. Bryce was not her friend. There would be no next season. Gabby stood. The walls were suddenly too confining, closing in.

She twisted the doorknob, opening it to see twenty-odd faces staring at her, eager for the gossip that they would surely theorize over well into next week. Gabby had always loved this place, this silly garage, but she knew that this moment would erase all the happy memories she had of it forever. Was there nothing Rachel Forrest couldn't take from her?

Somehow, her safety boots carried her past her now-former coworkers in a terrible blur and delivered her to her car.

"Gabby!" Talon's voice called, his own safety boots crunching on the gravel. They slowed as he reached her. "Please tell me he didn't cave to those bigots."

She didn't want to talk about this right now. She wanted to make it home before the reality of all this hit her like a speeding bus.

"You need to fight this. Wrongful dismissal. Take him to court, whatever it takes." His brown eyes were earnest, his hair falling into his eyes where he combed it to cover the worst of his acne.

Gabby sighed. "Right now, I just need to make it home."

Talon shook his head. "I could rally the others. We could all threaten to quit unless he hires you back."

She smiled despite herself. He was a sweet kid. But when she glanced at the old building, she knew one thing for certain. "I'm not sure I want to be somewhere that will get rid of me just because someone tells them to."

Talon quieted at that. He sighed. "You know, I only applied here because of you. My friend's older brother used to work here. He said you were a good ally, that you'd make sure I was safe."

Tears stung their way into Gabby's eyes. "Thanks, Talon. That's really nice to hear."

An air horn blasted from the shop, the signal to scramble into crews. Talon gave her a final, sad smile, and ran back to join them.

Gabby started her car. The drive home passed in a blur until she finally pulled into the driveway that wouldn't be hers for much longer and went inside the house.

Manny wasn't home. He was always at Derek's now, but Toebeans Morrison padded out to greet her. "Mrow," he said, simply.

Gabby stumbled past the cat, down the hall, and flopped onto her bed. She hated this feeling of detachment, even if she knew it was keeping a dark pit of her imagined inadequacies at bay. Some people raged and shouted, exorcising whatever toxins were building up inside them, but Gabby shut down, frozen deep inside her body, curiously detached and eying her situation from above, like a Rubix cube she couldn't solve, but couldn't look away from either.

At some point Toebeans Morrison climbed onto the bed, licking her fingers cautiously. When she didn't respond with the cuddles he'd hoped for, he padded up to her pillow instead, pulling her long hair as he kneaded himself a place to settle down.

His warm, furry body flopped around the curve of her head, his purrs vibrating into her scalp and slowly drawing her back into her body, where she closed her eyes and focused on his rumbling.

***

Eleven-year-old Gabby raced home as soon as she got off the school bus, hoping against hope, every muscle tight as she slipped through the slushy, salty muck on the side of the road.

Road grime caked the snowbanks in ugliness. A grey sky carried on the threatening mood, but she had to keep hoping. She willed everything okay. Maybe her mother hadn't gone into her room. Maybe she had tucked the contraband fantasy book she'd smuggled home from the book fair someplace safe after all.

The image on the cover--a kind lady faerie wielding a magic wand--flashed through her mind. She'd bought the book to stare at the image as much as read the story. It was like a perfect, special secret, but if her parents found it...

Gabby was still pulling her boots off when her mother stepped into the kitchen, her arms crossed. Gabby didn't need to look up to sense the tension in the room. Her fingers stalled on her boots. Gabby wished, not for the first time, that her life had a remote control that would let her pause and rewind back to the moment when she did something wrong. Then she could rewind back to this morning, put the book in her school bag, and come back. When she looked back at her mom, it would just be something small, like a chore she'd forgotten to do that she'd be in trouble for. Not something as big as a book.

"I found this in your bedroom. Do you want to explain to me how it got there?"

Gabby straightened slowly. No remote, then. The beautiful book was in her mother's hands, her face tight with fury. "A girl at school gave it to me," she mumbled. She couldn't tell the truth without getting in worse trouble.

"Who?" her mother demanded.

"Sarah," Gabby answered. There weren't any Sarahs in her class, but Mother didn't know that.

"You are not to associate with this Sarah anymore, understood?"

Gabby nodded. She wasn't allowed to be friends with anyone at school.

"You understand that books like this can bring demons into the house, don't you? Do you want our Bibles flying off the shelves, our dishes smashing onto the floor, all by themselves? Because that is what's going to happen." Mother glared, waiting for an answer. Electricity seemed to crackle out of her, reaching across the empty space to Gabby.

"No." Tears filled her eyes. She'd never get to finish the story now.

Mother softened, surprising Gabby. "I do understand the temptation. I used to read books like this too. Sometimes it's nice to escape our world for a little while, but they're not safe, do you understand? They will warp your mind."

"But they're just stories. I know they're not real," Gabby pleaded, swiping at her dribbling nose with her sleeve.

"Stories like these try to teach us that someone other than God will save us," snapped Mother, a stone wall slamming into place where the softness had been. Gabby knew that wall too well to bother trying to climb it. "They want you to think that heroes should be counted on, worshipped. They poison us into thinking that we can save ourselves. And what does the Blessed Scripture say about that?"

"Only god can save us," Gabby answered in a tiny voice.

"That's right. Good girl." Mother took her arm and led Gabby into the dining room where the fat woodstove that heated the house lived. Mother opened the iron door with a creak, revealing the flames inside. Wood smoke wisped out, acrid in Gabby's nose.

Oh no. Gabby knew at once what Mother intended to do.

But instead of tossing the book into the flames, Mother handed her the book. Bewildered, Gabby stared down at the beloved cover, the faerie smiling up at her like an old friend. She resisted the urge to hug it to her chest.

"Throw it into the fire," Mother ordered. "It's better if you do it yourself. It will purge the demons."

Gabby froze. No. She couldn't do that. She'd never forgive herself if she burned a book, especially this book, with her faerie friend on the cover. Something like that would leave a stain on her soul that she'd never be able to live with.

"Gabby. I wasn't asking."

Gabby couldn't move. She could hardly lift her chest to fill her lungs. She pulled herself deep into her mind, where no one could reach.

***

Gabby opened her eyes to a darkened room. Toebeans resumed his purring as he felt her shift and she reached a hand up to give him a scratch behind the ears. She sat up, swinging her legs over the edge of her bed.

She did feel better now that she remembered why this was all happening. Being punished, if that was even the right word for it, for doing the right thing wasn't anything new. She hated it, but there was a recognizable pattern to it in her life.

If she was a book she would call it a theme, but, ugh, she could really use a better theme, thank you very much.

She'd always hoped for a magical one, but at forty-five she supposed it was a little late to find it now. The best stories were reserved for younger folk and her younger years were consumed with surviving a cult and then trying to navigate the bewildering outside world she'd never been taught to understand.

Gabby rubbed her hands over her face and stared at the *Care and Feeding* book. At least she'd have time to read it now. With a small sigh, she reached for the skeleton key and tied it on to her wrist.

Her mood remained bitter and brooding after she'd brushed her teeth and washed her face, so Gabby decided to take a walk. She doubted Rachel Forrest would be out after dark to complain about Gabby using sidewalks or whatever right the woman would decide to strip from her next.

She pulled on a loose hoodie, keeping her long hair tucked in the back, and a ballcap to hide any feminine features. Another advantage of invisible middle age was being able to walk at night again, though Gabby did avoid certain areas of town.

She headed away from the Forrests' house, toward Tenth, where Ashlin's youth center lay. It would already be closed, but she wouldn't be surprised if Ashlin was still there.

The night air was cool and a low fog crept in off the river, carrying the earthy smell of the riverbanks to replace the asphalt and exhaust fumes of the day. So, she'd lost her job and her home. Sounded like the chance of a fresh start rather than an ending, she decided.

She shoved her hands into the front pocket of her hoodie. Yes, better to convince herself of that than brood over what it had been like being unhoused when she was sixteen. But Gabby had survived that, too. She had a car this time around, which was good, because she doubted

Toebeans Morrison would put up with life in a tent. Not with those claws of his.

Someone in a running outfit walked around the corner, minding their own business, eyes on the ground, clearing stewing over something. Gabby startled to see a book on their head, standing upright. *Leaves of Grass* by Walt Whitman. She did a double take, and the book disappeared.

"Excuse me," she said, before she could stop herself.

The walker stopped, casting her an expression that could only be a plea to be left alone. But something compelled Gabby. "Have you ever read Walt Whitman's *Leaves of Grass*?"

The stranger's brow knitted together, no doubt wondering why this stranger was raving about old poetry in the middle of the night. "No, "they answered.

"You should," Gabby gushed, unable to help herself. Was this some gentle form of psychotic break? "Most libraries will have a copy. I think it could change your life. If you read it."

Their bewildered look made her trail off. She hadn't read *Leaves of Grass* since she was fourteen, why did she suddenly have such strong opinions about it?

The stranger hurried along, leaving Gabby to collect her confused thoughts. "It's been a long day, you're entitled to weird book recs," she told herself, wondering if she should text Ashlin. Gabby could already hear what she'd say. "Okay, so you recommended some poetry to a stranger. I'm not sure that's anything to worry about, Mom. They probably thought you were high, but I'll bet they'll never forget the title of that book."

A daydream formed in Gabby's mind. The stranger, at a secondhand bookshop, coming across *Leaves of Grass* mis-shelved in science fiction. They didn't read poetry, hated it in school, but they 'd hesitate, thinking of that weird woman on the street. It would be enough to crack the cover open, take a peek. The book would take care of the rest.

Maybe she'd been reading a little too much *Care and Feeding of Your Little Banned Bookshop*. Gabby gave a nervous laugh that the darkened street ignored.

She turned onto River Road, so named for being backed by the river. She liked walking here. The street was always quiet, filled with the kinds of businesses that closed at five. The river kept its evenings foggy, and once in a while she would catch a glimpse of muskrats chasing each other in the shadows.

It gave her chest a sharp pang to think she might not live close enough to walk here in a month or so. She gave the road a wistful look, taking in the silhouette, the softly lit fog, and slowed her steps. The shape of the silhouette was wrong, somehow.

Gabby narrowed her eyes, trying to place the strangeness. There, just up ahead, a dark gap where the pattern of the streetlights faltered. What building was that? Gabby moved closer.

Didn't Gurdeep Optometry usually butt up against William's Law? Both businesses were housed in 18th century officer's quarters, from somewhere in the city's shipbuilding history. A front yard, a backyard, side walls shared with their neighbor, for hundreds of years. Only now it appeared as though another building had squished itself in between the two.

"Which is definitely not possible," Gabby murmured to herself. She should probably mind her own business, but she stepped closer instead, squinting past the streetlights that ruined her night vision. There was what looked like a shop window, so grimy that it failed to reflect the light. A second story peeked over a wooden sign. Gabby cupped her hands around the sides of her eyes to block out the streetlights so she could read it.

The Little Banned Bookshop.

Chapter 5

When you first meet your Bookshop, the experience can be bewildering. Most of us have much to learn about what is possible and what is not in this new reality. The Bookshop, however, does not comprehend concepts like denial and disbelief, making this introduction a tense time for your Bookshop. Please refrain from voicing thoughts like "this can't be real" or "I must be hallucinating" as these may confuse your Bookshop and make it question its existence.

- Care and Feeding of Your Little Banned Bookshop, page 11.

It was real. Leona's bookshop. The one in the book. It was all real. *And magic*, Gabby realized with a gasp of excitement.

A grin tugged at her face and she made short work of the space between her and the door tucked into an alcove on the right of the building. It was too dark to say for sure, but she thought the exterior was painted her favorite shade of dark green. Her hand clasped an antique doorknob, cold to the touch, and she held her breath as she twisted the knob.

The doorknob stuck, refusing to budge. Gabby jiggled it and tried again. No use. It was locked.

Gabby frowned at the doorknob. This wasn't how this sort of thing was meant to go. She'd found the impossible, magical bookshop against all odds. She couldn't just be locked out.

Gabby stepped backwards, peering into the darkened windows, Maybe someone was there who could let her in. No, this place was dilapidated. It had clearly been vacant for a long time.

She tugged at the old cobwebs along the panels of the wood as an inexplicable wave of sadness rolled over her. It was enough to know it existed, she supposed, even if she'd just stumbled into someone else's story. Girls like her, kids like Ronnie, they'd have this place.

She shouldn't be disappointed. She shouldn't. It had just been such a hard couple of days. Gabby sat on the curb, her back to the Bookshop, and put her head in her hands.

Maybe it was that book. The one her mother made her burn. Maybe the Bookshop had a rule about never letting someone who had burned a book inside.

Gabby ran her sleeve over her cheeks to brush away tears, the old key springing loose from her cuffs and catching her eye. Was it glowing? Faintly, for sure, but it was glowing. She'd worn the thing off and on for almost thirty-five years and it had never glowed.

Untying it from her wrist, Gabby turned it over. It was a skeleton key, after all, weren't they supposed to unlock everything? And the door handle was antique looking.

She took a deep breath. This was silly. But it was also too dark for anyone to see her foolishness. If she didn't try, she'd always wonder what would have happened if she did. Fine. She stood, turning back to the alcove. The faint light of distant streetlights revealed a lock plate above the doorknob. Gabby rubbed the key with her fingers before gliding it into the lock. If she broke off the H for hope she'd never forgive herself.

She squinched her face as she turned the key and held her breath. The lock mechanism clicked and the door beneath her hand swung open.

"No way," Gabby muttered, grinning to herself, but she hesitated. If she went inside, would that be trespassing? Breaking and entering?

A light switch lay just beyond the open door. "Hello?" She called out. "Is anybody here?" She flicked the light on. It flickered once, twice, before settling into a warm, yellowed glow.

Dusty cobwebs stretched from wooden bookcase to wooden bookcase, all of them stuffed with books. Gabby reached out and traced her fingertips along their spines, leaving a long line in the dust. What had happened to this place?

Layered rugs, once with rich Persian designs, led a worn path from the door to the counter. She supposed that was where people could ask for their one book.

Gabby stepped farther inside. A small staircase tucked behind the counter peeked out from behind a dark green wall panel that doubled as a door. On the other side, before the grimy window, sat a trio of inviting red velvet chairs.

She touched them gingerly, testing their plumpness as a plume of dust lifted into the air. A chair like this needed a cat. Toebeans Morrison would happily volunteer. "Not that I'd want to impose," she said aloud to the Bookshop.

It was real. It was all real. But it was also a mess. "I'm not sure I'm allowed to be here or who owns this building, but if you want people coming into this bookshop, you're going to need to clean up a bit," she said aloud.

The lights dimmed and the shelves seemed to sag, almost imperceptibly. Or more likely, her imagination was getting the better of her.

"I could help, if you want, "she found herself saying, "I mean, not that I have any particular skills in the matter, I've never trained as a professional cleaner or anything." Gabby stopped. "Sorry, I'm really nervous, I guess. I've never met a magic bookstore before. But I have found myself with a lot of free time on my hands, so, I don't know. If all the cobwebs and dust are itchy, I could help with that."

The lights brightened and a slow creak jostled the dust motes as a hidden door opened in the wall behind the counter. Gabby opened the door wider and peered inside. A feather duster, a vacuum, broom, window cleaner and some rags. Nothing of the industrial products she remembered from working in fast food restaurants back when she was first on her own. That was probably a good thing.

She reached for the duster, its handle painted the same dark green color as the walls. It probably wouldn't work with this much dust. Manny always said these things just tossed the dust into the air to settle down again the moment you thought you were done.

Still, it matched the bookshop and it was the only duster here. Gabby held on to the feather duster and surveyed the shop. Where to begin?

She opted for the shelves nearest the front door. First impressions were important, after all. She recognized many of these titles: *The Hate You Give, I'm Not Dying with You Tonight*. Modern books, mainly Young Adult. Maybe that's why they were shelved nearest to the door, though surely if the books were shelved by publication date, rather than author last name, they would be impossible to sort. Unless, of course, they were added as they were banned. The duster tickled over the spine of *Maus*, grabbing at a cobweb in the corner of the shelving.

The dust motes in the air didn't grow thicker, and the feathers didn't gum up with sticky spider silk the way they should have. Gabby slowed, feeling a vibration in the soles of her feet, a barely perceptible rumbling at the edge of her hearing.

Was the bookshop *purring*? The book hadn't mentioned anything about purring, but Gabby supposed that she hadn't read the whole thing yet, either. A grin tugged at her lips.

Twenty years ago, Gabby might have grumbled over the idea of discovering an actual magic Bookshop and then cleaning the damn thing instead of doing main character stuff, like running the place. Saving it from certain doom. Helping it through an existential crisis, things like that.

Gabby had already had her story, and it sucked, but she'd survived. And she'd mellowed enough, she supposed, to be content as a side character who helped the bookstore tidy itself in preparation of meeting their new shopkeeper. *Who knows?* She had the book and the key, after all. Maybe there was a smaller role ahead for her in this story.

Still. A part of her couldn't help feeling a bit like Molly Grue in *The Last Unicorn,* lamenting that the unicorn never came to her when she was still young and beautiful. Gabby scowled, wondering if being trapped in a cult and the psychological aftermath of unraveling a lifetime of cultural conditioning had used up Molly Grue's best main character years as well.

Gabby moved deeper into the bookshelves with her long thoughts. Metal labels were fastened directly to the wood with tiny screws. Gabby read one as her duster cleared it of clogging debris.

Nalanda Mahavihara, it read. She frowned at the books. They looked new, freshly bound, but there was something ancient about that name. Something familiar, but just out of reach of her memory.

She switched the duster to her other hand, letting her eyes wander through the bookshop. The ceiling had panels that probably gave an illusion of depth. Cheery, but small chandeliers offered a warm light that spilled over the shelves. Maybe too warm to light up the nooks and crannies of these shelves the way they did.

Gabby chuckled at herself for critiquing a magical bookshop's lighting. Why shouldn't that be magical too, after all?

She moved to another shelf, her gaze flicking to the metal label. *Institute for Sexual Research*. Gabby pulled the duster back and hugged it against her belly. Leona had told her about this place; they had studied alternate sexualities in the 1900's.

She could almost hear Leona admonish her, "Honey, they did a lot more than that. They performed the first gender affirming surgeries."

Gabby reached out with her free hand, close, but not quite touching the books for fear they'd disappear. "The Nazis gutted it when they were in power. One of their biggest book burning bonfires was that library.' Leona's eyes had glistened as she shook her head. "All that knowledge, gone."

But there were copies here. And the *Care and Feeding* book had definitely established that there were more than one Little Banned Bookshops.

Gabby stepped back until she felt the press of the opposite shelf in her back and leaned against it. If this was possible, what else was possible in this place?

One thing was certain, this place should never have been allowed to get this dusty. "Why was no one looking after you?" she asked aloud.

Again, a slight dimming of the lights. "Did they pass away and leave you alone?" She reached out and stroked a shelf soothingly as the lights grew dimmer still.

Gabby moved to the open section, some nonsense logic insisting that the library could hear her better there. "Don't worry. If the magic managed to send me here to get you cleaned up, I'm sure your shopkeeper's on their way too." Gabby frowned. "Maybe they're a germaphobe. Or afraid of spiders." She hadn't actually seen any spiders, though. Just cobwebs.

A light over the bookshop counter came on, sending a soft sunbeam of light onto the counter. Dust motes twinkled as they drifted through. Gabby blinked as she noticed a book on the counter. Had that been there before? She moved over to it. She knew that book. It was sitting on her night table at home.

Care and Feeding of Your Little Banned Bookshop.

Gabby picked it up. Odd that this copy had the same creases on the cover that hers did. She opened the book as she saw the bookmark poking up. Her bookmark. It was one of thousands Ashlin had made for her when she was little. Tattered and faded now, but something Gabby treasured. This was odd.

"Yes," she said to the Bookshop. "Your new keeper should be getting a copy, just like me. I'm sure they just haven't had the chance to read it yet."

The Bookshop's lights dimmed. Gabby sighed, if this kept up, she'd be dusting in the dark. "Don't worry! In the meantime, you've got me."

She gave the counter a rub with her knuckles. Come on, Gabby, it's not a cat or a dog. But the Bookshop brightened again, the low rumbling returning.

Gabby and her feather duster returned to work, *Care and Feeding* safely stowed in Gabby's hoodie. *The Women's Library of Atlantis* announced the shelf's label. Atlantis! Again, the books were bound in a modern fashion, though she supposed they should be scrolls or clay tablets.

Would the bookshop mind if she just had a look? She carefully drew out a cheery blue book. The color was solid, the title embossed, simply, in gold leaf. And English. Which made Gabby frown. That wasn't right.

She leafed through to the first page, where began the story of a pinecone merchant who spent her days climbing trees and dreaming of becoming a bird. Gabby had the sneaking suspicion a god might actually turn the woman into a bird by the end of the story. Soon, it seemed that was the story. Girl, unsatisfied with her life, turns into a bird, gets lonely, misses her family. Goes back. That old universal story.

Gabby squirmed. She hadn't gone back. Stay a bird, be free, she urged. Her stomach rumbled, pulling her out of the story with a craving for pine nuts.

"Sorry!" she gasped, realizing that she'd been reading when she was supposed to be cleaning.

The bookshop rumbled. It looked better, somehow. Not just the dusting, it looked healthier.

She looked back at the book in her hand, finally piecing things together. "Oh! You were hungry, weren't you? Wow, you really do feed off the energy of people reading, don't you?"

The lights flickered. Gabby set down the duster. "Do you want me to read some more? So you're not hungry?"

The light over the counter came on again and a new book appeared. Gabby grinned, making her way over.

She sucked in her breath when she saw the cover: a kind faerie lady wielding a magic wand. Gabby could hear her heart beating in her ears as she reached for it. The edges were singed black. *No, it can't be.* Gabby held her breath as she opened the front cover. There it was: *Sarah*, written in a fake, clumsy hand so her mother wouldn't recognize Gabby's handwriting. Tears rushed to her eyes as Gabby hugged the book. "You saved it?" she finally managed to ask.

The Bookshop rumbled softly.

Gabby stepped over to the nearest bookcase and threw her arms around the side of it in a hug. "Thank you."

Gabby opened her eyes, her body strangely cramped. She wiped moisture from the side of her mouth, trying to figure out where she was, because this was decidedly not her bedroom. A book slipped from her lap to the ground with a thump. The Bookshop. She was in the Bookshop.

Disoriented, she retrieved the precious, singed book and hugged it to her chest. She sat up, frowning groggily through the front window. Now the sun was up, she could see just how thick the grime had gotten. She walked over to it, brushing her thumb against the glass. It came back blackened with dirt. Gabby didn't know how a window could get that dirty.

She softened. Unless the bookshop didn't want anyone to look inside.

Gabby turned back to take in the shop. It looked better than it did last night. Cleaner, though she doubted that was thanks to her efforts. The chairs were clean, the carpets less worn. Hmm. She pulled *Care and Feeding of Your Little Banned Bookshop* from her pocket, flipping to the Table of Contents and searching for cleaning. There it was. Page 202.

Little Banned Bookshops are primarily self-cleaning, but keepers should be aware that self-cleaning uses up tremendous amounts of the Bookshop's energy. If you notice that your Bookshop is growing dusty, this is an early sign of undernourishment. Please take care to spend at least two hours a day reading. After cleaning, the next function to go is food preparation.

Happily, the Bookshop always stores enough energy in its reserves to deliver books as needed.

Gabby turned the page, her mind filling with questions, but the next page was blank, followed by the start of a new chapter. She flipped back to the original page. If she understood this correctly, the Bookshop was only messy because it was starving? A pang of guilt that didn't make any sense stabbed at her heart. "I'm not awake enough for this," she said aloud.

At the sound of her voice, the Bookshop came to life and the smell of coffee filled the shop. Not just coffee, but her coffee. Coffee was the one snobbery Gabby allowed herself. A particular brand of dark roast, ground to a fine dust and brewed in a French press for at least ten minutes.

Gabby stepped away from the shelves, following the scent, and sure enough, there on the counter, sat a French press, beside a steaming mug that read *I Heart My Little Banned Bookshop* in red letters. She bit back a smirk at the cheeky mug.

"Thank you," she told the bookshop, taking a sip and finding the coffee to be the perfect drinking temperature. *I could get used to this*, she thought. Aloud, she said, "I have to go home, to feed my cat and have a shower, but I'll come back after. You just need someone to read, right? Doesn't matter who? Because I can do that."

The lights brightened, and a small bowl of cat food appeared on the counter.

"Oh, thank you, but that's okay, I've got plenty of cat food at home for him." She cocked her head. "It's not just hungry, is it? You're lonely too, aren't you?"

The cat food vanished, save a few crunchies. She took that as a yes. "Could I bring my daughter and my friend

Manny to see you? They're safe people. I'm supposed to have dinner with them tonight, and I'm not sure they'll believe me if they don't see this with their own eyes."

The lights flickered. Nervously, Gabby thought.

"I'll come back and read all afternoon, that way you should have lots of energy to clean up with. Would you be less nervous, then?"

The lights grew brighter and soon Gabby could feel a rumble beneath her feet.

Gabby took a deep breath as she slid the key into the Bookshop's lock, a part of her afraid that it wouldn't work, that this had all been some fever dream. But the lock clicked open and the Bookshop's light revealed a cozy, clean space.

"Wow. It's just like Leona described it. It smells like books and cinnamon." Manny grinned at Gabby, his eyes filled with wonder.

Gabby gave a discreet sniff. It did have a cinnamon scent now the dust was gone. She bit back a smile. Thanks to all her reading.

"This is exactly what a magical bookshop should look like," Ashlin stared into the Bookshop, her mouth a round O. Of delight or surprise, Gabby couldn't say for sure.

Ashlin's gaze settled on the red chairs and frowned. "This place needs a cat."

The lights glowed brighter, sending a nervous flutter into Gabby's belly. This was a lot. Manny and Ashlin cheerfully accepted the building appearing from seemingly nowhere. But explaining how the Bookshop communicated, that felt... private was the first word that came to her. No, that word wasn't right. Too far, maybe. She rubbed her palms on her jeans. She hadn't been this nervous since she'd first met Ashlin's father.

Manny walked up to the counter. "May I have my one, true book?"

Gabby shook her head, ready to explain that the bookstore wouldn't be able to give out their books until the Shopkeeper arrived. She stopped herself as a book appeared on the counter.

Manny's laughter rang out through the Bookshop. "Look at that."

Gabby must have read that chapter of *Care and Feeding* wrong or misunderstood it. Somehow. She supposed she should have been reading that book, but the Bookshop had rescued the faerie book from actual flames for her. She didn't want the Bookshop to think she didn't appreciate that.

"If that's a sex manual, I don't need to know," said Ashlin, holding up her hands.

"Derek should be so lucky," Manny shot back, grinning over his book. He glanced up, meeting Gabby's eyes and held up the book. *A Year in Arcadia: Killerion.*

"Have you ever read it before?" Ashlin asked, clasping her hands with excitement.

Manny shook his head. "I haven't," he said, his voice growing thoughtful. "Strange to know in advance that a book will change your life when you read it."

"Okay. My turn." Ashlin gave him a playful shove and faced the counter, clearing her throat and clasping her hands as if in prayer.

Gabby looked away, suddenly uncomfortable. Did she want to know what book it would give Ashlin? What if--a horrible thought gripped her--what if Ashlin's book was one of the Beholder's texts. Panic gripped Gabby's heart. Like some genetic trick of cults that skipped a generation.

"Oh, I read this one in college and loved it!" exclaimed Ashlin, her face curdled bright red.

"How naughty is it that it's making you blush like that? "asked Manny.

Gabby put her hand on her chest, her heart beating wildly with relief.

"It's not naughty, not like that. *Carmilla*. It's this really old, Gothic lesbian vampire story that I read to, um. Impress a girl."

Gabby gasped. "Not THE girl!"

Ashlin hugged the book to her chest and nodded, eyes bright.

"Wait. I feel left out." Manny pretended to pout. "Who is THE girl?"

Gabby waited for Ashlin to tell him, absentmindedly rubbing the nearest bookshelf the way she'd absent-mindedly rub Toebeans Morrison's belly when she was reading.

"I met her in university, then we got jobs in different cities and long-distance sucks, so we ended things. But. She called me up last month to let me know she's moving here and wanted to make plans to meet up," Ashlin explained in a rush.

Manny lit up. "Oh my god, we're having a double wedding, I know it."

"Whoa." Ashlin held up her hand. "Way too soon for that, Mr. Man."

Manny pretended to pout, drawing more laughter from the girl.

Ashlin peered over at her Gabby, clearly eager to change the subject. "So, what's it like being a magical Shopkeeper?"

Gabby blinked. "Me? I'm no Shopkeeper. I'm just feeding it in the meantime."

Ashlin furrowed her brow. "But didn't you tell me the Bookshop needs to have a keeper, that they work together? You're the one who found the book."

"And you had the key to the place since you were a little girl." Manny's brow creased as well, giving the two of them a matching set of disapproval.

"No, I don't think so," insisted Gabby. Girls that burned books didn't grow up to be magical Bookshop keepers, even if the Bookshop saved the book in the end. "I'd know, wouldn't I? Besides, I'm not a teenager."

Ashlin cocked her head. "I'm not a hundred percent sure teenagers are the best people to run magical bookshops, Mom."

"Yeah, that sounds like a terrible combination," added Manny. "Why teenagers?"

Gabby shrugged. She didn't know how to explain her weird thought processes. "It just seems like becoming the keeper of a magical bookshop is main character stuff, you know? So, therefore, young people, making their way in the world."

"Okay, but what if this is your story? Surely you get to be the main character in your own story?"

Gabby didn't love the thread of concern she heard in Ashlin's voice. "I just think that I might have a mentor role in this one," Gabby said slowly. "And I'm good with that."

Manny wrinkled his nose. "Mentors usually die, don't they?"

"Manny!" Ashlin swiped at him and squinted at the nearest bookshelf before releasing a gasp. "This says the Library of Alexandria!"

Gabby silently thanked her for changing the subject again, when a door, hidden in the walls, creaked open, revealing a brightly lit staircase. Her heart thumped in her chest. She knew it was the Bookshop who opened the door. Was she going to meet the shopkeeper at last?

"What's up there?" asked Manny, stepping over to peer up the stairs.

"I think that's where the Shopkeeper lives," answered Gabby, her breaths coming shallow. She fought the urge to pull him back into the public areas of the Bookshop.

"Have you been up there yet?"

"No, of course not." Gabby shook her head. "Imagine if they're in there, sleeping or showering or getting dressed and I just turn up in their apartment."

Manny shrugged. "Just tell them you had the key."

Maybe bringing them here had been a mistake. Gabby just wanted to share the magic with them, not argue about keys and roles. There was a strange, fragile balance here that she worried might snap and banish her from the Bookshop forever.

"What do you think will happen tomorrow when the businesses reopen and discover their new neighbor?" called Ashlin, still exploring the shelves.

"I don't know." Gabby rubbed the counter comfortingly. "The Bookshop can leave. It can move. It should move, that's what keeps it safe and able to give out books." *Please go somewhere safe*, she mentally urged the Bookshop.

Ashlin chewed her lip. "Do you have a way of finding it again if that happens?"

A deep sense of loss opened in Gabby's chest. She shook her head.

CHAPTER 6

Gabby sipped at her morning coffee, watching Toebeans Morrison nibble at his breakfast of kitty kibble. She'd had a fitful sleep, shifting from worries about how the business sector was going to react to finding the Bookshop this morning, to worries that the Bookshop wouldn't be there to be seen and she'd never see it again.

Toebeans looked up at her and mewed.

"I suppose it could make itself invisible," Gabby answered as if she understood. "But then I wouldn't be able to see it either."

Toebeans blinked slowly.

"Yes! You're right, the book should tell me.' She dug out *Care and Feeding of Your Little Banned Bookshop* and checked the table of contents. "No, there's nothing about invisibility."

Gabby set the book on the counter and reached for her coffee. She propped herself up on her elbows, coffee in hand, and took a sip before leaning her cheek against the mug. "I read a section the other day which explained that if the Bookshop is waiting for its Shopkeeper, it will wait as long as it takes, even to its detriment," she explained to the cat. "What do you think is taking them so long?'

Toebeans Morrison met her eyes briefly before washing his face with his paw.

"You're right. I've never been a terribly patient person, have I? At most, people are going to gawk, make a fuss, maybe fine it for unpaid property taxes or something. It's just hard not to equate this Bookshop with our Little Free Library, bullied into nonexistence." Her gut clenched at the thought.

Toebeans walked over and waited for Gabby to give him a scratch under the chin. He purred loudly as she complied.

"The Bookshop is probably getting hungry, too. I should go check on it." She felt a pang of guilt for spending so much time there, rather than home with Toebeans. But he was also used to her working landscaping hours. A part of her wanted to bring him, just to have the satisfaction of seeing a cat curled up on the Bookshop's chairs.

If the Bookshop was still there.

A moment later, she was tugging on her shoes. She went on foot, half-expecting a crowd if the Bookshop was still there and not trusting herself to drive if it wasn't. Her pace quickened at the thought, her mind refusing to consider what she'd do if it was gone. She clutched at the key and felt for the book in the pocket of her hoodie.

As she turned the last corner, tears of relief pricked at her eyes to see the Bookshop still there. It was early, not quite eight, and the business folk were just beginning to arrive. A bearded man took pictures of the Bookshop, and as she watched, someone she recognized as Ashlin's optometrist joined them, gesturing at the Little Banned Bookshop.

Maybe she could still protect the Bookshop from whatever was coming. Or, at least, give it some advice about self-worth and Shopkeepers who were taking too long to show up.

Gabby pulled her hood over her head and tucked herself inside, careful not to look across the street at the photographer. Her hands shook as she gripped the key, untying it from her wrist to unlock the door quickly.

She took a deep breath as she passed the lawyer's offices and turned quickly into the alcove of the Bookshop's entrance. The door swung open on its own, as if the Bookshop had been waiting for her.

Once inside, Gabby released a deep breath, reaching out to one of the shelves for support as the adrenaline that had carried her past the photographer and the optometrist subsided. "Good morning, Bookshop," she said aloud.

A mug of coffee appeared on the counter. *I Heart My Little Banned Bookshop,* it announced, making Gabby grin for the second time.

"Thank you." Gabby curled her hands around the mug. "I was a little worried you wouldn't be here this morning."

She turned to face the window, glad for the grime that kept the Bookshop's interior shielded from view. "You've probably got more experience with this than me, but."

The Bookshop waited.

"Are you safe?" She wished her voice didn't sound so anxious.

The Bookshop didn't answer. Gabby sighed. Maybe the Bookshop wasn't sure either. She glanced at the grimy window. There must be a reason the Bookshop hadn't cleaned it, after all.

Gabby pulled her copy of *Care and Feeding* from her pouch and sunk into one of the cozy red chairs, balancing her coffee. "It's peaceful right now, so let's get you fed in case I'm too distracted to focus later, "she explained aloud.

The lamp beside her switched on and she settled into the book, turning to the chapter on Bookshop safety.

While it might be difficult to suppress your concerns over the Bookshop's welfare, please be assured that the Bookshop has been in operation a much longer time than you might expect. It is very capable of looking after itself.

In fact, the only time that the Bookshop is truly vulnerable is when it does not have a Shopkeeper.

Gabby suppressed a sigh and squirmed in her seat. That was what she worried about.

Because the Bookshop needs a Shopkeeper to give out book s...

Gabby sat up. She hadn't read that wrong after all. She glanced back at the door that hid the stairs. Had there been a shopkeeper here all along, hiding up there while she cleaned and fed the Bookshop? She frowned. That didn't seem very Shopkeeper-like.

But then she considered the stories she'd read. Main characters always took a few chapters to come round to believing in an impossible, mythical situation, didn't they? Nobody is going to come across a magical Bookshop and say, "Yes, this is a real thing that is happening. I'll drop everything and become a Shopkeeper."

Gabby frowned into her coffee. Maybe she was meant to speed that process up? A mentor ready to take their hand and say something along the lines of "yes, this is all very real and it's time to live up to your magical responsibilities."

She returned to the book, finding her place on the page.

Because the Bookshop needs a Shopkeeper to give out books, it will remain in the place where it has planned to meet said Shopkeeper until the Shopkeeper claims them.

Gabby considered the words, reading them over and over again. A good mentor would guide this claiming, to help keep the Bookshop safe. She lifted her head. "Do you have any books on how to be a good mentor?"

Gabby lost track of how long she'd been reading when she returned to reality sometime later, drawn home by the small but gathering crowd outside the Bookshop. She glanced at her phone. Almost noon. That sounded about right for word to spread and onlookers to arrive.

She peered through a clean spot in the glass. "There's a news crew setting up," she explained to the Bookshop. "They're probably going to do a story to ask if anyone knows how you got here. Magic isn't so easily accepted by the majority of people, I'm afraid."

The lights dimmed and she reached out to rub the windowsill.

"Sorry, that wasn't meant to hurt your feelings. It's just that we've all had a rather rough decade." Gabby sighed. "Magic's been in short supply." She glanced back into the Bookshop, her heart catching with the affection she'd developed for the place so quickly. "Though I suppose that's why you're here, huh?"

A fresh, steaming mug of coffee appeared on the counter. Gabby smiled, stepping away from the window. This Bookshop certainly had her figured out. She sipped her coffee, watching the obscured shapes of the news crew setting up their shots through the window.

"Thing is, what are they going to say about you? I mean, besides the way you appeared over the weekend. It would be nice if you had some control over the narrative."

Gabby thought back to her beloved Little Free Library. Her heart fluttered. She couldn't bear to go through that again, not if there was some way to protect the Book-shop. To tell its real story before someone else jumped in with a false one. Her stomach turned to imagine what Rachel Forrest would say about this place. Should Gabby go out there? She glanced down at herself. Clean pants, not jeans, nothing stained from work, and she'd worn a button-down shirt under her hoodie. She was presentable, if nervous. "Should I go out there?"

Rather than brightening, the lights warmed, going from white to a rosy orange color that felt immediately cozy. Gabby clutched her coffee mug. *I Heart My Little Banned Bookshop*. And she did, after all, even if this was the sort of thing that terrified her. She couldn't let anyone sully the story of Leona's magical Bookshop the way they did her Little Free Library. Gabby set the coffee down and squared her shoulders.

With a small creak, the Bookshop opened the front door for her. Gabby took a deep breath and stepped out into the sunlight, pausing for a moment to let her eyes adjust.

When they finally did, a half-dozen pairs of eyes looked at her. Gabby stared back, holding her breath. Set an example, Mentor, she urged herself, but her body refused to move.

A reporter in black heels and highlighter-pink lipstick stepped toward her, holding out a microphone. "Excuse me, ma' am, did you just come out of this building? Do you work there? What can you tell us about it?"

The questions came at her fast as bullets. Gabby glanced back at the Bookshop, looking lovely as it basked in the noon-time sun, and gave herself the moment to collect herself. She could do this. For the Bookshop.

"I am a friend of the Bookshop," she told the reporter.

"What does that mean? Is that like the Friends of the Library association? Do you know where this building came from?"

Gabby closed her eyes. Control the narrative, protect the Bookshop. "I'll do my best to answer your questions," Gabby told the reporter, reaching for the microphone and releasing a tiny sigh of relief when they handed it over.

She turned to the camera. *Don't think about it, just talk.* A cold sweat coated her body. She opened her mouth, but nothing came out. *Oh no.*

Be the magic bookshop you want to see in the world. The idea filled her with courage. Maybe the Bookshop sent a little magic, she couldn't be sure, but for the moment, Gabby wasn't afraid. "I first heard about the Little Banned Bookshop a few decades ago, from an older friend. Leona. She explained to me that the Little Banned Bookshop travels all over, appearing to those who need it. And if a person finds the Bookshop open and unlocked, they can go inside and request their one, true book. This book is said to be a book that will change their life forever. Maybe it will help them find their true selves, recover from trauma."

Gabby looked back at the Bookshop, her heart suddenly bursting with pride. "Discover something important. Maybe it's a book that will help them change their lives. Maybe it's a book that will let them know they're not alone."

She paused there, and the reporter leapt in to fill the gap. "How does the Bookshop know what book to give?"

"It just does. By magic, the stuff of legends, I don't know how to explain that."

"And when you were just in there, did you get a book?"

Gabby shook her head. "No, sorry. You see, as I understand it, the Bookshop's been away for a while. I think it was resting? But lately, with the recent rash of book banning, it's returned. When I saw it, I remembered the stories, so I've been cleaning it up, getting it ready to meet its new Shopkeeper. Once they arrive, then I believe that the Bookshop will be giving out books again." She hoped that was right, she was still confused on that part.

"Can you explain how this building just appeared here? Earlier this morning, surveyors were measuring the property lines and somehow their instruments failed to measure any of the space that this Little Banned Bookshop takes up at all. They've plans to return with different equipment, but for now it appears that the Bookshop doesn't take up any space at all. Can you explain that?"

Oh, that was fascinating, but Gabby shook her head. "Like I mentioned before, I was told this is a magical Bookshop. It appears where it is needed. Maybe it exists outside of space?"

"So you're saying this is an actual magic Bookshop." The reporter went over and slapped her hand on an exterior panel. "Feels real to me, folks."

Gabby crossed her arms, resisting the urge to ask the reporter to keep their hands to themselves. *Well, if everyone believed in it, it wouldn't need to disappear and reappear again*, she reassured herself. She needed to regain control of the conversation. "The Bookshop is hope," Gabby said. "Sure, it gives us our life-changing book and maybe that improves our lives, but it also keeps the books safe."

The reporter gave her a predatory smile. "Can we see inside?"

No, was Gabby's first instinct, but that wasn't her place. "That's for the Shopkeeper to decide, once they arrive."

The door of the optometrist's office opened and the bearded man scowled in their direction. The reporter rushed over. "Mr. Gurdeep? What have you got to say about the statement that this building is home to a magical bookstore?"

Gabby took advantage of the news crew's shift in attention to duck back inside. She leaned against the Bookshop door as she closed it behind her. Clutching her trembling hands together, Gabby exhaled slowly, her mind already racing with things she should have said differently, with ways she could have sounded more clever, more polished.

"I think I'm going to need some chocolate," she joked aloud. Even her voice trembled. It was like the confidence to speak had come from somewhere else and now it was gone, she felt spent.

Gabby let out a surprised laugh as a bar of chocolate appeared on the counter. She crossed the room in a few quick steps and nibbled at it gratefully. "Hopefully they won 't edit everything I said into something else," she told the Bookshop. "Ideally, they'd refer to me as a local wierdo and air my interview as a bit of local color."

It only took a few hours for the first texts to come in. *Saw you on the news!* Gabby searched for the clip on her phone, playing it with the volume up so the Bookshop could hear it, too. As she'd hoped, they'd included everything she said with a small disclaimer that the news station couldn't verify the use of magic.

She was curious what the Bookshop's neighbors thought of it all. "I'm skeptical of the magical aspect, but I don't see anything malicious happening," said Mr. Gurdeep. "Our building appears untouched, though I will be verifying that with the building inspector."

"And how would you feel if this Little Banned Bookshop were here to stay? "asked the reporter.

The optometrist crossed their arms. "As long as the owner applied for the appropriate permits and pays their fair share of taxes, I don't foresee any problems."

Gabby winced. She doubted the Little Banned Bookshop existed as a corporate entity and refused to offend it by asking. She turned the phone off.

Unable to sit still any longer, she paced the length of the Bookshop, worrying about the practicalities of all of this. With a sigh, she retrieved the duster from the tiny closet just to have something to keep her busy. She peered out the window more than once, and there was no denying the growing crowd, cell phone cameras trained on the Bookshop.

Finally, Ashlin sent her a text. *Check out #TheLittleBannedBookshop. It's trending EVERYWHERE.*

Gabby set down her duster, sinking into a cozy chair. She brought up the only social media she had left and typed in the hashtag. 547 results. Gabby leaned forward, how was that possible? It had only been a few hours! She skimmed through the results, many of which were just reacts to posts on the news reel.

Gabby played a few videos of book girlies gushing with delight over the idea of the Little Banned Bookshop so the Bookshop could hear. She smiled as the lighting took on a rosy hue. "Are you blushing?" she teased the Bookshop, which led to the rosiness deepening.

"I actually found a Little Banned Bookshop in the 90's," said a woman at the beginning of one reel. Gabby turned up the volume, eager to hear more. "I was in my 20's and visiting San Francisco for the first time, boggled by everything and, you know, doing all the cheesy, tourist things that people do."

She had a raspy voice and deep laugh lines that made Gabby like her immediately. "At first, I didn't realize that this Bookshop was different from any other Bookshop. There were still lots of independent bookshops back then. Except, when I went inside, it felt different, you know? Like there was magic in the air. My mama always told me I had a special sense for things like magic, and this time, she might have been right. I mean, how often do we encounter magic in our lives to test a theory like that?"

The woman gestured broadly, her colorful collection of silver bangles clinking cheerfully against each other. "The

Bookshop was filled with shelves, just like you'd expect, but something drew me to the counter and just compelled me--I don't know what else to call it--to ask if it had a book for me."

The camera zoomed into her face. "And this book just appeared on the counter." She held up her arm. "It still gives me goosebumps all these years later. And you can bet I still have the book." She held up a well-loved copy of *The House on Mango Street.*

"Did it change my life?" She chuckled. "Hell yeah, it did. Reading it on the plane ride home from that trip led to an introduction that unlocked a whole series of events beyond the scope of a short video."

The woman smiled at her book. "You know, one thing no one's mentioned yet is that the Bookshop gives you your book. It doesn't matter if you're a pauper or a prince, you'll get your book. That part of its lore has always meant a lot to me."

Darn. Gabby should have mentioned that when she was talking to the reporter. That was an important detail.

Her finger scrolled through the next few videos. An excited-looking youth filled the screen. "You won't believe this! I'm visiting my Great-Grandpa and he says that he actually found the Little Banned Bookshop in Paris when he was younger!"

The camera panned to an older man with thin white hair on a hospital bed, an oxygen tube running into his nostrils. "Yes, I remember that day well. I was looking for that famous bookstore. What was it called again? Oh yes, Shakespeare & Company. But I found the Little Banned Bookshop instead." He gave a short, raspy laugh. "There was a fella in my platoon, Cutter was his name, who told me all about it one night when we were holed up under this bridge.

"I thought he'd made it up until I saw the bookshop for myself more than twenty years later." The man's voice caught. "Of course, we lost Cutter in Normandy. Hadn't thought of that legend of his since the war, if I'm honest. Not until it was right there in front of me.

"Had to go in, of course. Anything less would have been disrespectful to his memory. But first I stood outside, looking up the sign. Of course it was in French, you see. Gave it my best salute and went inside."

"What book did you get?" urged the great-grand child.

The elderly man's chuckle turned into a cough that went on for some time. Finally, he gave the camera an exhausted nod. "I tell you what, I don't think I'll share that with the whole world, but if you ever get the chance to meet that Bookshop, please tell it old Albert says thank you."

Gabby looked up from her phone to make sure the Bookshop had heard. The lights remained the same, but her feet tickled as its rumbling purr returned.

"You probably don't often hear from your clients after the fact, huh?" The thought made her sad. No wonder *Care and Feeding* described the Bookshop as lonely. So many lives changed, but so far removed, the Bookshop could only trust the books had worked their magic.

She rubbed the arm of the chair. "Don't worry Bookshop. I'm not going anywhere." But even as the words left her lips she wondered if that were true. Eventually the true Shopkeeper would be here and Gabby would have to leave without any guarantee of seeing the Bookshop again. She wished that... Gabby shut the thought down. There wasn't any point wishing for something that wasn't meant for her.

Biting back a sigh, she scrolled deeper. "Can we just talk about how awesome it is that this bookshop exists?" a young, heavily made-up woman with perfect hair gushed. "Ya'll better be messaging me the address if you find this place."

Gabby scrolled on. "I think what I like best about this magical Banned Bookshop is the hope I felt when I first heard about it," a sincere-looking youth with the handle of Non-binary Dan said in the next video. "Because, if you think about it, its existence takes away all of the power of these book banners."

Gabby settled back in the chair to listen. "At the heart of book banning lies this fear that someone will read something in the books they're banning that will threaten the book banner's ideals or way of life. Sure, they'll all say it's 'for the children' or whatever, but really, they're just terrified that if the status quo shifts, they'll lose their power. So, they take away these voices, these books, that pose threats. To keep people like me small, to keep my voice from growing louder. And now we know that there is this receptacle of the world's banned books that will give you one of them for free. That's just amazing." They placed their hand on their chest, eyes misty, clearly overwhelmed.

Gabby followed their account immediately. Hope. She rubbed the H of the teeth on her key.

Leona had told her once that "hope and joy are the best tools against fascism. They want you to be sad and worried and miserable. Hopeful, joyful people show others what life can be like. They're contagious. They spread, just like all that toxic junk does. Only they lift people up rather than bringing them low."

Gabby pictured Leona standing in the Bookshop, looking around at the books. "I wish you could be here," Gabby whispered. It didn't matter if the Bookshop could hear her or not, she'd only said it aloud for Leona's memory to hear.

The memory winked at her and took a long drag off her empty cigarette holder (she'd quit the addiction, but never the habit. It added such drama, after all). "No matter how down you are, you keep smiling, my girl. Just to piss off the fash."

Gabby's phone dinged with a text from Manny. No words, just a link that opened to another video, one that Gabby hadn't seen yet, from someone named Gwenthebookshopper. A red head with a mass of cheery curls grinned at Gabby from her phone.

"Listen, I have no way to prove this and it doesn't matter if you believe me or not, but my Aunt was actually a Shopkeeper at one of these Little Banned Bookshops. I say one, because she told me they were all over the world and that they show up wherever they're needed."

Gwen tucked her hair behind her ear. "My aunt also told me that the Bookshop and the Shopkeeper have this really important relationship and she actually looked after the Bookshop so it could do its important book-giving-away work." She giggled. "Sorry, not the most poetic way of putting it, to be sure. And anyway, the shopkeeper stays with the Bookshop for the rest of their life. My aunt came to visit on holidays and whatnot, but that Bookshop was her home and weirdly, it also kind of seemed like her best friend?"

Gwen's eyes grew serious. "She passed away about a decade ago. I really miss her. But you know what strikes me as funny now? It never occurred to me that this might not be real. I've never seen the Little Banned Bookshop and neither has my mom, but we never even considered that my aunt's stories might not be true. Of course, now that I know it's still out there, I may need to go find it for myself."

Maybe this Gwen is the missing Shopkeeper. The thought brought with it a mean sprig of jealousy. Gabby frowned at her phone. That was no way for a mentor to react. She clicked into Gwenthebookshopper's profile. The woman's videos were mainly about bookbinding and book repairs; hobbies that Gabby had to admit would be handy for a Shopkeeper. Maybe Gabby should message her. Nothing untoward, something subtle, just a hint in the hopes it might trigger a positive reaction.

Hello there. Gabby typed out with her thumbs. *I'm actually the woman from the newsreel about the Little Banned Bookshop that recently appeared. After viewing your video about your aunt, I'm hoping you might have some answers for me. I think that I am the Banned Bookshop's Shopkeeper's mentor. They haven't arrived yet, so I'm looking after and feeding the Bookshop until their arrival. The thing is that I'm getting worried that the Bookshop is in danger if they remain in place much longer and I don't know how to find the Shopkeeper I'm supposed to mentor.*

I do have the book, but it doesn't offer any help in this situation. Did your Aunt ever mention anything about her mentor and how they found her? Any clues or details you remember would help me out a great deal. Thank you!

Gabby read the note over with a sense of satisfaction. This was clever. If Gwen was the Shopkeeper, this should help her realize and if she wasn't, she still might be able to help.

It was growing dark when Gabby hit send. She peered outside, the crowd having grown. She pulled her fingers into nervous fists and stretched them out again. She didn't want to go out there. Someone could follow her home, or worse, think the Bookshop empty and break in.

"May I sleep here tonight?" she asked the Bookshop.

The door to the stairs creaked open. "No," she said, her palms held up. "That wouldn't be right. Maybe just a cot down here, and a few blankets?"

A cot appeared at once. A moment later, so did a plate of spaghetti. Gabby hadn't realized how hungry she was until she smelled the sauce. "Crap," she said, realizing that

Toebeans wouldn't be fed. "I need to get someone to look in on my cat."

"Mrow," called the cat, padding down the stairs and into the Bookshop proper.

Gabby stared. "Oh. Kay," she said, confused, as Toebeans Morrison rubbed against her ankles. She closed her eyes. Magic bookshop, she reminded herself.

Chapter 7

The Little Banned Bookshop has always had its enemies and detractors. Some of them make very good arguments and hold influence over others. As a rule, the Bookshop themselves give little stock to these people. It's tempting to believe that this suggests the Bookshop is impenetrable, but even magic Bookshops can crumble. As Shopkeeper, however, you need to recognize the threat these individuals hold. Usually, these people will be revealed by their book, before their actions can cause physical harm to the Bookshop. A blow to one Bookshop can echo through the others.

- Care and feeding of Your Little Banned Bookshop, Pg. 168.

"I always knew you'd disappoint me," Gabby's mother told her. "But making goo-goo eyes over Beelzebub's Bookshop? Really Gabby, why don't you just slap your father and me in the face?"

Gabby groaned. She'd had this nightmare before. *It is possible that I do things for myself for reasons that have nothing to do with you.*

"Technically, there's a whole school of psychology that would say otherwise."

Wake up Gabby. You're just arguing with yourself. It's not worth the dreamspace.

"What are you doing wasting your time here?" her mother continued. "Even the Bookshop doesn't want you. It knows you'll just abandon it the moment your faith is tested, because that is what you do."

My faith wasn't tested. I never had any. I didn't believe in the mean, hateful deity you kept insisting was loving and I wasn't willing to give up my chance of a happy life just to keep up a charade that, quite frankly, wasn't fair to impose on a child. Wow. She wished she could articulate herself this well in the waking world.

"But you have no problem believing in a so-called magical Bookshop. Humph. Held together with demon semen, no doubt."

Gabby shook her head. It was an expression she'd grown up with, but it was also such a messed-up thing to say to a child. *And you think the Bookshop is the problem.*

"Look at how deeply they've ruined your mind. Turned you against us." Gabby's mother went on. "You can't ever escape us, you know."

I know. The room filled with balloons. Gabby and her mother pulled out pins and automatically began to pop them the way they'd once folded laundry together. This was usually the part of this nightmare where the popped balloons would reveal that they were inside the old Beholder's church, and Gabby would be staring into the blue weave of the chair in front of her again, shutting down to save herself.

Instead, the balloons began to float upwards, revealing the Bookshop. Gabby held the pin in her hand, still.

"Tsk tsk tsk." Gabby's mother shook her head. "God isn't going to like this."

Gabby squeezed her eyes tight. *Hope. Yesterday had been filled with hope.*

"Hope? There's a heavy price to pay for that. Good feelings are how you know you're sinning. Silly girl, you'll never feel good without eternal punishment to follow."

"Enough!" Gabby shouted. "Why would you choose to live that way? You could have chosen literally anything else.

Something that didn't expect you to disown your child just because they wanted to live their lives in a way that didn't feel like a lie. Then maybe you'd have some right to judge me."

Her mother wavered, her eyes darting back and forth. "Quiet down. It's disrespectful to talk to your mother like that."

Gabby rolled her eyes, then stopped, looking back at her mother. Above her head sat a book. *How to Raise Faithful Children Who Do What They're Told.*

The fight drained out of Gabby. Imagine if her mother had gotten that book at some past Bookshop. Imagine if she'd read it and it changed the course of her life, if it had kept Gabby from straying from the Beholder's Pathway to Righteousness. If Gabby had been the perfect daughter, sacrificing herself to fulfill her mother's dreams.

How narrowly had Gabby escaped that fate? Was her eventual excommunication really her decision or some trick of luck that kept a book from her mother's hands? Gabby shuddered. The balloons bloomed into roses and bumped against the ceiling. She squirmed. *I don't like this dream. Wake up, Gabby, or dream of something better.*

Gabby awoke to the smell of books and old wood, an explicable sense of relief coming over her as she opened her eyes. Across from her cot, Toebeans Morrison lay curled up in one of the red chairs, looking as perfectly at home as the cat Gabby had first imagined there. She reached out to rub his ears and he rolled over in his sleep, his purr starting up immediately.

The Bookshop, noticing her movement, offered a coffee. "Thank you," she said, getting up and walking around to the far side of the counter so she wouldn't spill any on the cot. *This is nice.*

The Bookshop looked different from this angle. It had a vantage point where the bookshelves didn't cut the view of the shop as a whole. Gabby straightened, sensing the importance of the Shopkeeper's vantage point for a moment, only to slump as she remembered that it wasn't her vantage point, after all.

She moved to take a sip of her coffee, only to miss and slop some down her shirt and onto the floor. "Oh! Sorry!" she told the Bookshop, bending down to clean up the drops with her sleeve.

The cupboard beneath the counter was an open cubby and from her odd angle, Gabby noticed a signature peeking out from a stack of notebooks. *Emily Smiles.* Now that was a main character name if Gabby had ever heard one.

She pushed the notebook aside, looking for more. *Kevin Somers* read another, with the note, *raised two kids here!* Gabby ran her fingers over the signatures. These must be the Bookshop's old shopkeepers, signing this cubby as a way to make it known that they were here. *Todd Bellview. Annalee Anders.*

She should write these names down, do some research on their lives and how they came to be Shopkeepers. Maybe write a little biography companion to *Care and Feeding of Your Little Banned Bookshop*. Gabby smiled. That way, a part of her would always be here.

She greedily took in more of the names, committing them to memory, until she reached a familiar signature that made her breath catch. *Leona Trivitz.* Gabby stared, her hand covering her mouth. That was her Leona's name. The one she and Manny had named their Little Free Library for. But Leona didn't live above a bookshop. Gabby and Ashlin had visited her in her little trailer dozens of times.

Gabby turned to the door leading upstairs, still open. It was a magic Bookshop, after all. What if Leona's trailer was up there somehow?

Leaving her coffee behind, Gabby stepped through the door, holding tight to the railing as she went up the full flight of stairs.

Her heart pounded as she reached the top. But this place was nothing like Leona's trailer and it was clear that no one lived here. Not yet.

The unfurnished apartment had windows every chance it could, looking out into a leafy, green space. There was something oddly familiar about it; some nostalgia, like the daydream of an apartment Gabby had dreamed of as a child, before practicalities and budgets came into play. Airy windows, dark walls, rounded doors. She looked to her left and saw a small library room, complete with a rolling ladder. "Geez, living in a Bookshop isn't enough?" she said aloud, hands grazing the ladder.

But her eyes kept going back to the windows. Something wasn't right. All at once, she realized it. River Road wasn't treed. And there couldn't be windows on the sides because those sides were joined to the historical row houses.

Gabby found the front door and wrenched it open, stumbling out into the sunlight of a quiet, country road. When she looked back to the place, she saw a neat, blue cottage with the numbers 331 beside the door. "Where am I?"

She swallowed hard to stem the rising panic and stepped back inside the house, locking the door firmly behind her. She forced herself to walk calmly down the stairs again.

She held her breath until she found the Bookshop waiting at the bottom of the stairs. Gabby closed the door behind her, releasing a small sigh of relief as her eyes found Toebeans, still curled up on the chair where she'd left him.

Her hands trembled as she reached for her coffee, thought better of it, and walked to the front door of the Bookshop. She had to know. The door opened easily, and Gabby blinked at the sudden sunlight. River Road waited outside, just as it always had.

But magic aside, how could the top of the bookstore be in a different physical space than the Bookshop? Gabby took a few steps across the sidewalk and peered up at the second floor. Here, the sign obscured the lower portion of the windows. When she was upstairs, nothing had blocked the windows.

Gabby desperately wanted to understand this. Why? Unless, maybe this was to give stability to the shopkeepers? They would have a fixed address, like Leona's trailer, someplace for friends to visit. Gabby furrowed her brow. Gwenthebookshopper clearly knew all about her aunt. Why hadn't Leona told them about her secret life as a Shopkeeper? Had Gabby proved herself untrustworthy somehow? She would have loved this -- she would have leapt at the chance to be so close to magic like this.

But then, Leona had always kept her secrets. Life had taught her to be like that. Gabby pulled the key from her pocket and stared at it. Had Leona recognized the key? And if she had, then...

Gabby's thoughts were interrupted by a minivan pulling up and screeching to a halt. Rachel Forrest glared at Gabby from the driver's seat, her eyes narrowing.

Gabby stared back. What was Rachel Forrest doing here?

Rachel pursed her lips. "I should have known you'd be a part of this," she hissed. The door behind her slid open and several women with picket signs spilled out.

Didn't we already play this game? Gabby wondered, keeping her body between the crew of Rachel's evangelists and the Bookshop.

A book appeared over Rachel's head. *How to Ban Books and Influence School Boards.* Gabby squinted, trying to make out the author. By what sense of irony was that published as a book?

"What are you staring at?" snapped Rachel.

Gabby shook her head. She certainly wasn't going to share that title with Rachel and give her more fuel for her anti-book campaigns. *It's probably not safe to stay out here, either,* a voice in her head insisted, bringing Gabby back to her senses. She had enough experience with the Beholders cult to know she wouldn't be convincing anyone to change their mind today.

She turned, light-headed, and reached for the door. The handle refused to give and Gabby stared at it a few seconds before she realized it was locked. Which was no big deal, she had a key, after all. It was just that the Bookshop had been so gracious about opening doors for her of late that this felt strangely purposeful.

Perhaps Gabby should have lingered long enough to figure out why, but she'd tangled with Rachel Forrest before. And lost everything. Gabby fumbled with the key, finally opening the door and rushing to shut it behind her.

She leaned against the door and slid to the floor, staring ahead without seeing, turning the key over in her hand. Now Rachel Forrest was after this Bookshop, too.

"Listen, Bookshop. Please. That woman out there, she's awful. She started this whole campaign to get rid of my Little Free Library because her teenager got a book from it that she didn't approve of. She's probably the antithesis of everything that you stand for. But she's dangerous, you understand? She got me kicked out of my home and fired from my job."

The lights in the Bookshop flickered and the bulbs buzzed with electricity.

"I'm not saying she's stronger than your magic, but please. Make sure she's worth the risk of staying here before you get hurt."

The Bookshop's floorboards rumbled.

"What if you go to that pretty treed place I saw upstairs? I can stay here, wait for your Shopkeeper to show up, and then bring them to you. Wouldn't that be safer?"

The lights dimmed. *Silly, stubborn Bookshop.* If anything happened to it, it would be her fault now. Whatever malice Rachel held for books, it would be tenfold now that she'd seen Gabby.

***

Gabby's father glared at her, arms crossed. His public grief over, fury emanated from him in electric waves. "You've ruined your life, you know. No good man will marry you now."

Gabby tugged her backpack on. She bit back a whimper. *Please, Dad, just stop talking. Let me get out of this without any further damage.*

"You have no idea how to survive. You're too naive to understand how the world works. You're going to fail and fail spectacularly. You'll probably be raped before the week is out and end up a prostitute. The police are going to show up with pictures of your murdered body, needles sticking out of your arms, expecting your mother and me to come identify your body in some morgue."

That was absolutely not going to happen, Gabby reassured herself. She wouldn't let it. She stared at his shoes. *Please Dad, this might be the last thing you ever say to me. Can't you think of anything kind to say?*

"You are going to fail at everything you do." Gabby's father shook his head. "And when you do, I want you to think of this moment."

***

Gabby didn't like to think of how often that parting curse had resurfaced in her memory. She checked her notifications to see if Gwenthebookshopper had messaged her back yet. Anything to distract herself from that memory. No such luck.

She sat with her back to the window so she didn't have to see the shadows of the picket signs Rachel and her evangelists wielded outside. Not seeing them didn't mean she couldn't feel them out there, like some phantom itch. Spoiling the pleasantness of the Bookshop with their toxicity. No wonder Manny had called her when they were gathering around the Little Free Library. As far as she could tell, they weren't picketing actual libraries yet, but they certainly seemed to be making their way in that direction.

Focus on your book, Gabby. You need to feed the bookshop. She struggled to get into her book. It was impossible to relax, let alone focus, knowing Rachel Forrest was just on the other side of that wall.

Gabby wished Leona had told her stories of the Little Banned Bookshop. There really should be a book in here about that. Or even a whole series of books chronicling the Bookshop's adventures. Now *those* books Gabby would be able to read in times of crisis.

Heck, she could have written them, if she'd been the Shopkeeper. Then the next Shopkeepers would have a few extra tools at their disposal. She could even write books on Bookshop Lore for the fans the Bookshop had found online.

Gabby released a sigh that made Toebeans Morrison come over and settle into her lap. She would have made a great Shopkeeper.

Gabby shook her head and put the book down. There was no use reading if she was just going to spiral. She checked #TheLittleBannedBookshop instead. Rachel had had plenty of time to spread her own version of events, after all.

The topic had only picked up speed overnight, ballooning to almost a million videos. Rachel Forrest wasn't the only Christian to oppose the Bookshop, either. They were coming in force simply to condemn the magic behind the Little Banned Bookshop.

"It isn't magic. This isn't some fairy tale. This is the work of Satan himself, using his demons to create a receptacle of smut..."

Gabby flicked to the next one video, marveling at just how unhinged those once-familiar arguments became when the viewer didn't share that worldview.

Eventually she scrolled onto a video by Rachel herself. "It's no surprise to me to discover that known groomer, Gabby..."

Gabby swiped past, to find a reaction video to the same. A brown-skinned lady in a golden crown, ball gown, and shimmering eye makeup gestured to the video Rachel had made in a side-by-side shot. "So, I did some digging into this and it turns out that the only evidence of 'grooming' by our Bookshop friend Gabby stems from this Rachel's accusations."

She leaned closer to the camera as Rachel's side of the screen switched to the video of Gabby getting out of the Mulvaney Landscaping truck. "Apparently, before she brought us all in on the legend of the Little Banned Bookshop, Gabby had one of those Little Free Library boxes in front of her house that held some LGBTQIA + literature. For years. Then this Rachel person moves into the neighborhood, freaks out, calls up her church posse, and they all start picketing this woman's house. She even finds out where this power ally works and gets Gabby FIRED when she starts this whole campaign calling her a groomer for having some friggin' books in a box." The ballgown lady widened her eyes and shuddered with exaggerated shock.

Gabby sank deeper into her chair. Hearing her recent troubles spelled out like that, and so publicly, was unexpected.

"So, let's be clear, this Rachel woman and her entire account is WILD. It's all about hating on books and trying to get queer lit banned from everywhere. And apparently, ruining this poor Gabby person's actual life."

The other half of the screen shifted over, allowing the sparkling woman to fill the screen. She held up a finger with an intimidatingly fancy gel nail as she made her point. "This kind of woman is exactly why I, for one, am glad that the Little Banned Bookshop exists. And as for Gabby, I've got your back, girl. The villains aren't going to win."

Gabby put her phone down, a slight smile forgotten on her face, staring at the chair across from her as she gathered her thoughts.

A violence of sudden sound struck Gabby's eardrums and she flung herself to the floor. Toebeans raced up the stairs. Was that a gunshot? "Are you okay?" she asked the Bookshop, her voice shaking, ears ringing, knee scuffed from her descent.

The lights dimmed. The front window had spider-webbed around a brick still lodged in the glass.

Gabby got to her feet, her limbs trembling from the fright. Maybe she should see her doctor about blood pressure medication after all. The longer she stared in disbelief at the ruined window, the more she understood that the Bookshop had been hurt. She couldn't say whether reading could fix this or not. *Care and Feeding* didn't contain those chapters, because the Shopkeeper was supposed to be here so the Bookshop could avoid danger.

Fury came next. After everything Rachel Forrest had done, her appetite for punishing those she decided were in the wrong, with all her self-righteous dogma, this was a step too far. Gabby flung open the door and marched outside.

She met Rachel's eyes first, who offered a smug smile. It didn't matter if it was Rachel or one of her minions who had thrown that brick, they both knew whose muscle had been behind it.

"Hey!" shouted the lawyer from next door. Williams something or other. His face was red with fury. His eyes darted from the brick to the picketers. "Destruction of private property does not make your cause look any better, Mizz Forrest."

Rachel shrugged. "Oh, that? That wasn't us. This mess of a woman here did it, saying she was going to make it look like it was us." She adjusted her hold on her purse. "As if anyone would believe that God-fearing women like us would do such a thing."

Gabby was speechless. The very idea that she would hurt the Bookshop appalled her.

The lawyer walked over and stood beside Gabby. "I can assure you, ma' am, that that kind of lie will not serve you well in court when I offer the footage I'll retrieve from the security cameras placed on both my building and the businesses across the street. You see, we watch out for each other here on River Road and wanted to make sure we had every angle covered."

Gabby glanced at him. Then he had footage of everything, the Bookshop's arrival, her crying on the curb, her glowing key.

"In fact, I'm sure the police are already on the way. Do you have a permit for this impromptu protest?"

Rachel sizzled with helpless rage, squirming like bacon in an overheated pan. "There was a crowd here all day yesterday and nobody minded."

"Ah, but they weren't bothering the clients of River Road businesses. In fact, they attracted new customers and gave us invaluable positive exposure online. Your little group, on the other hand, is engaging in property destruction."

Gabby watched Rachel, frozen now with rage, in awe. A part of her wished that she could have inspired that kind of response, even though she knew full well half of that was a lifetime of religion grooming Rachel to be subservient to men.

This wasn't over. Rachel would just refocus and come back with new tactics. *How to Ban Books and Influence School Boards* bobbed above Rachel's head.

Gabby looked away, only to see more books above the heads of Rachel's friends. She hesitated over the woman wearing a silver cross with *A Munich Manual of Demonic Magic* over her head. There were more Bibles attached to the group than Gabby knew what to make of. Her head spun. She closed her eyes for a moment before turning back to the lawyer.

He watched the women pack up their things with crossed arms and a calculated glare. Dostoyevsky's *Crime and Punishment* rested above his head. Gabby tried not to stare.

The brick lodged in the window pulled her attention away. She hesitated to touch it lest the whole window come crashing down, but it didn't feel right to just leave it there. Was there some sort of Bookshop First Aid she should do? She was so tired of waiting and not knowing how to keep this special place safe. And so tired of Rachel effing Forrest ruining everything Gabby loved.

"I'd leave that, for now." The lawyer gestured to the window. "Take some photos for your insurance company. If the Bookshop has one. Or leave it as evidence for the police, if you want to involve them."

"I'm not entirely sure the Bookshop is legal, sir," Gabby answered. She regretted it right away. That probably wasn't something she should have said to a lawyer.

He handed her a business card. "I met a similar Bookshop in my youth and it helped me immensely."

His eyes were soft as hers widened. How had the Bookshop's reach been so great, but no one ever talked about it?

"Should the Bookshop ever have need of a lawyer, I'd be honored to help."

CHAPTER 8

As a Banned Bookshop keeper, I like to believe that there is a book for everyone searching. Yet, every so often someone is discovered who we do not have a book for. Either their issue is too narrow, too new, or the client's situation too unique to have a single solution. In these situations, the client is offered any available Bookshop as keeper, in the hopes that this security will give them the opportunity to survive, live good lives, and possibly to write the book they might have needed for the next seeker.

- Care and Feeding of Your Little Banned Bookshop. Appendix B. Page 236.

The rest of the afternoon passed peacefully, allowing Gabby to feed the Bookshop while eying the damaged window, hoping to see it repair itself. No such luck.

"Does it hurt? "she asked aloud.

Did the shadows in the Bookshop deepen? Why was the Bookshop being so quiet?

This was her fault. Rachel Forrest would never have set her sights on the Little Banned Bookshop if she hadn't seen Gabby. Part of her knew that wasn't entirely true, but she wasn't in the mood for logic as dusk fell on the awful day. At least it would be over soon.

Her phone trilled with a text. *Mom, can you come walk me home? Someone called in a threat to the center. It's probably nothing, but just in case.*

Gabby stood, mom powers activated. She wasn't interested in anyone else she loved getting hurt today, thank you very much. Ruffling Toebeans' ears with a pat, Gabby peered around the shop, wishing it didn't seem so wounded.

"Will you be okay if I slip out for a bit?" she asked aloud.

The light over the counter flickered. Gabby wasn't sure what that meant.

"My daughter needs me to get her home safe, but I'll come back after. Is that okay?"

The Bookshop seemed so sad. *Dammit Shopkeeper, where are you?*

Gabby locked the door behind her, wishing this didn't feel wrong. What else could she do? She couldn't abandon Ashlin to real danger because of imagined danger, could she?

The street was quiet but for the crickets on the riverbank. In the distance a trailer with an excavator strapped to its back sat on the side of the road.

Gabby pulled up her hood and hurried through the dark streets. The youth center was only two blocks from River Road, but it seemed suddenly far now that she was worried about Ashlin.

What if Rachel had discovered that Gabby had a daughter and decided to terrorize her as well? What was next? Every friend Gabby had ever had? Gabby let out a barely concealed sob as she hurried along. Why did Rachel have to bring Ashlin into this? She chewed on these thoughts until she arrived at the Center.

I'm downstairs, she texted Ashlin.

A moment later Ashlin, alive and well, appeared and unlocked the door to let her in. "Thanks Mom." Ashlin gave her a quick hug as her phone trilled. "Its Manny," Ashlin said. "I texted him too. I'll let him know you're here now so he stops worrying."

She put her phone away a moment later. "I have just one thing to finish up, do you want to come upstairs?"

Gabby followed. The Center seemed different at night, without the usual energy that filled the place, the TVs gone quiet from whatever video game the kids were into these days, the computer screens dark. It still had that lingering smell of teenaged boy and cheap perfume, though. Gabby smirked, remembering her own beloved bottle of Malibu something or other.

She leaned against Ashlin's office door and opened her phone while she waited. They had an understanding, if Ashlin was scared or uncomfortable in this place alone at night, she was to call, no matter how much paperwork might be left. If Gabby wasn't available, she'd try Manny. All kinds of kids came through here, and not all of them angels. That being said, Ashlin rarely called for help. Something must have gotten to her. Like Rachel Forrest got to Gabby.

She should try not to make assumptions until Ashlin had a chance to explain. Gabby checked her messages to distract herself.

She sucked in her breath. Gwenthebookshopper had gotten back to her. *Oh, that's exciting! Sorry to disappoint, but my aunt never mentioned anything about a mentor. In the story she told me, she found a key and then a book on how to take care of the Bookshop. I forget what it was called. Then she said she started seeing books on people's heads?? Haha. Wild, I know.*

Gabby's fingertips grew cold. Books on people's heads.

"Hey Mom, I'm ready."

Gabby blinked at Ashlin, not registering. Ashlin grinned brightly and held up her keys.

Gabby followed her downstairs automatically, lost in a fog. No, it couldn't be. Could it? Surely *Care and Feeding* would have mentioned the books. *Gods, I must be a fool.*

They stepped outside and two dark shapes stepped from the shadows as Ashlin turned to lock the door behind them. Gabby moved in front of Ashlin. "What do you want?" she shouted.

"Crap! Sorry!" One of the shadows moved into the light. "I didn't mean to scare you."

Gabby sagged with spent adrenaline. "Ronnie? What are you doing here?"

"You know this person?" asked Ashlin, her hand halfway in her purse, no doubt clutching bear spray or something of the like.

"Hey Gabby," said the second shadow, the light revealing his face.

"Talon? You two know each other?" asked Gabby. Ronnie blushed as Talon shrugged and took their hand.

Oh, thought Gabby. *Oh.*

"Do either of you know about a certain threatening phone call I got this evening?" Ashlin's voice was firm.

Ronnie ran a hand through their hair. "Was it a woman? Sort of prim, but mean sounding?" When Ashlin nodded, they went on. "It might have been my mum. She's been coming kind of unhinged."

"That's why we're here, actually. We didn't know how to reach you and Ronnie remembered that your daughter worked here," added Talon.

He looked worried. Why did he look so worried?

"Then what's going on?" asked Ashlin.

"Listen, you have to understand that my mom thinks she's doing the Lord's work. She's convinced that God wants her to go on those weird crusades of hers. Only she's going way too far."

Gabby shivered, wishing they were back at the Bookshop.

Ronnie struggled to explain themselves further. Talon touched Ronnie's arm. "I'll do it." He gave Gabby a nervous smile. "They overheard her renting an excavator. Apparently, murder is the bigger sin, so she was going to get you out of the building and then use this rental to tear down the Bookshop."

Gabby stared at Talon, struggling to register what he'd said. Maya Angelou's *I Know Why the Caged Bird Sings* winked from above him.

"She wanted a wrecking ball, but they don't rent those out to just anyone, apparently," added Ronnie. They clasped Gabby's hand. "I'm sorry."

Gabby glanced at Ashlin. *Carmilla*, the book, floated just above her hair. " "I need to go," she said, dazed.

"Yes, Mom, run! I'll call Manny. We'll be right behind you."

Gabby's feet listened even as her mind struggled to register. There had been an excavator parked on the street when she left. It was only a few blocks. *Oh no! Toebeans is in there. The Bookshop is in there. Maybe the Bookshop's magic will protect them.* Breath coming hard now, legs pumping. *Don't trip, please don't trip. No, it can't protect itself. Not without a Shopkeeper.* It couldn't even protect itself from the brick lodged in the window. Gabby's hands pulled into fists as she wondered if that brick was the one that gave Rachel the idea. Her stomach turned, from the idea or from the sudden exertion, she couldn't say.

A car screeched up beside her. Manny's car. *Where did he come from?*

He leaned over and opened the passenger door. "Get in!"

Gabby didn't question it, getting in and pulling her seatbelt on, numb all over. "Manny. I think I might be the Shopkeeper, after all."

He kept his eyes on the road. "Yeah, hun. We've all known that for a while now. Figured you'd come around eventually."

Sirens whined in the distance. *Who called them? Will they be on the side of a Bookshop of banned books or the evangelist trying to destroy it?* Sweat trickled down Gabby's temple, cooling against her hot check. She wanted to cry. "What if all of my ridiculous trauma from the cult kept me from seeing this until it's too late?"

"Gabs." Manny's voice was soft, soothing. "It's not too late. Look."

Police cars, sirens blaring, their lights throwing chaos against the dark, filled the street. *Maybe the lawyer called them. Maybe all of his security cameras alerted him to Rachel's plan.*

Gabby got out of the car, walking into the chaos. Rachel Forrest was indeed there. She'd driven the excavator off the trailer and had the bucket lifted high, poised to rip into the roof of the Little Banned Bookshop. Did Gabby see the Bookshop cringe beneath its shadow?

The police officers leapt from their vehicles, guns drawn, a few of them gesturing at Rachel. "Get out of the excavator ma 'am. This is private property."

Another held up a hand to Gabby. "Stop right there, ma 'am. The police are handling this."

Another officer pulled out a roll of yellow ribbon and started taping off the area. Gabby moved into the forbidden area. "My Bookshop and my cat are in there!"

A female officer gave her a nod and pulled out a megaphone. The diesel engine of the excavator drowned out their voices. Rachel seemed to have frozen in place, as if she hadn't considered this happening.

Ashlin, Ronnie, and Talon arrived a few houses down, out of breath and leaning forward. Gabby waved, but the officer with the yellow tape cut them off.

"You okay?" Ashlin mouthed. Gabby nodded, relieved to see Manny walking over to join the younger folk.

"Turn the excavator off and step out of the cab, ma' am. At this point, you haven't done anything wrong. Come with us peacefully and let's keep it that way."

Gabby watched Rachel. The woman was clearly torn. She turned to the officer with the megaphone. Gabby couldn't hear what Rachel shouted, but she could read lips well enough to understand. "This bookshop is evil and God Himself has tasked me with its removal!"

Gabby shivered. Was Rachel actually willing to get shot over this? That wouldn't make her some sort of warrior martyr like she'd been taught; it would just make her dead. Gabby's stomach turned. How many times had the Beholders insisted that their members be willing to endure persecution, even death, because it guaranteed some sacred place for their souls? She knew at once that Rachel would happily die to destroy the Bookshop, even as the excavator's tracks moved closer to the building.

She was out of time. This was happening. "No!" Gabby's voice rang out over the road and the river. "'That's MY Bookshop!"

The lights in the Bookshop all came on at once. The broken window straightened, pushing the brick harmlessly to the sidewalk as the spider webbed glass smoothed into a single pane. Gabby locked wide eyes with Toebeans Morrison through the glass, stretching on his red velvet chair inside.

Rachel Forrest did not slow, no doubt doubling down on her intent to destroy the Bookshop. But the Bookshop wasn't helpless anymore. Gabby had finally claimed it. She grinned, a giddiness in her chest and tears in her eyes. *Main character feelings.*

The building lifted from its false foundation with the sound of tearing paper. Gabby gasped as it stood up on what she would later come to think of as four huge ele-phant legs.

Suddenly, the police officer's guns were no longer trained on Rachel, but the Little Banned Bookshop. "What the hell is that?" someone shouted.

Gabby could only stare.

An entire book dedicated to *Care and Feeding of Your Little Banned Bookshop* and it neglected to mention that the shop had legs? Unsteady legs, it seemed, or perhaps it had just been sitting too long.

Rachel, however, was unimpressed. Gabby noticed the tick-tick-tick of the tracks on pavement as Rachel plowed on, bringing the teeth of her bucket down into the roof of the Bookshop. Only they didn't bite into the Bookshop at all. They simply went through the bookshop without effect, as if the building was made of vapor. Meanwhile, the Bookshop stepped through the crowd, like a fright-ened child determined to reach Mom at all costs. Its door swung open and Gabby leapt inside as it scooped her up.

The shop turned around briefly, long enough for Gab-by to see the space between the optometrist and the lawyer gone, and Rachels' excavator lodged into the bro-ken roof of the lawyer's office. A few bullets glanced off the window.

"Ashlin's out there!" Gabby shouted in alarm.

The Bookshop leapt over the police cars to open its door a second time. Manny and Ashlin leapt inside without hesitation, turning back to reach for the others. "Come on!"

Talon jumped, landing inside, his wide eyes meeting Gabby's. He gave her a goofy grin.

"Seriously?" asked Ronnie, only making the jump after a bullet pinged off a nearby parking meter. Their foot caught on the carpet and they sprawled across the floor as they landed. The Bookshop shut the door after them and Ronnie groaned, their face pale. "Did we just get eaten by a bookstore?" they asked in a thin voice.

"Yes," answered Manny without hesitation. "But for the record, I was the most delicious."

The Bookshop leapt once, twice, and then the chaos and flashing lights of River Road fell away. Were they flying?

Ashlin and Talon helped Ronnie to their feet. "Are you hurt?" asked Ashlin.

Gabby waited to see them shake their head before going to the window. There was darkness beyond, but it didn't matter. She traced her finger along the healed glass, not caring if she left a smudge. "I just need to reassure myself that you're okay," she whispered.

Tsk, tsk. Now you're talking to a building well within earshot of other people. What will they think of you? she could hear her mother say. But, for once, Gabby didn't care.

Beyond the window, the cloud shifted, uncovering the Moon and revealing a clearing by a forest lake outside. The Bookshop's door opened with a sound like a sigh and the chirp of crickets and croak of bullfrogs spilled inside.

Ashlin chuckled. "That was wild! Did you see its legs? It's like a Baba Yaga hut, but with elephant legs instead of chicken legs."

Of course, thought Gabby. *Bookshops are heavier than huts.*

Ronnie and Talon exchanged glances. Ronnie shook their head. "No one's ever going to believe this story when we tell them."

Talon flopped onto a chair, stretching out his feet and putting his hands behind his head. "Tell them anyway. Life's too dull to keep something like this to ourselves."

Gabby smiled to herself, rubbing the windowsill with her knuckle and looking out at the dark lake. "Is this your safe place?" she asked the Bookshop.

The ripples in the lake caught the Moon's reflection and tossed it back and forth. Somewhere a barred owl hooted. Gabby grinned, imagining her younger self wandering around the wood and coming across a Bookshop in a clearing by a lake. Like something out of a fairy tale. In fact, as she glanced back at the softly lit shelves, she was fairly certain that had happened a few times already.

"I'm sorry it took me so long to figure this out," she told the Bookshop.

"Figure what out?" asked Ronnie, their eyes bulging as they squinted at a silver label on one of the shelves.

"I guess I just couldn't accept that something like this could happen to someone like me." The lights turned rosy, as if the Bookshop were glowing. Gabby kept her hand on the counter as it finally sank in.

"You're the Shopkeeper," said Ashlin, her eyes misty, her smile soft.

"Yeah," said Gabby. "I am."

For as long as books are banned, the Little Banned Bookshop will be out there, sometimes disguised as a library, sometimes as a story tucked into the folds of a book. Sometimes the person you thought was a librarian was a Shopkeeper all along. And one day, the Bookshop hopes it will find you and deliver to you the book that you need. Make sure you're watching for it.

- The Lore of the Little Banned Bookshop: A Handbook for Readers, Gabby's second draft, page 203.

ABOUT THE AUTHOR

Jennifer Shelby is known for hunting stories in the beetled undergrowth of fairy-infested forests. She fishes for them in the dark space between stars. As part of her ongoing catch-and-release program, a collection of these stories, *Borrowed Wings and other stories*, will soon be available.

If you'd like to get to know Jennifer better, or just keep up with her upcoming stories and books, please subscribe to her newsletter at https://authorjennifershelby.substac k.com

Acknowledgements

This book would not exist without Matthew LeDrew's writing class and workshop. Matthew's encouragement and especially his excitement about this story as I was writing made it possible for me to keep true to the dream of this book even as I worked through my difficult experiences of being in and leaving a cult.

Special thanks to Peter J. Foote, who beta read not only this novella, but the original short story that grew up to be this book. Thanks for always being there to bounce ideas off of and answer panicked publishing questions, Peter.

To my beta readers Nancy S. M. Waldman, Quinn Rin Croft, and Kerry Anne Campbell, thank you for the invaluable advice, for catching a kazillion typos, and for your encouragement.